THE WITCH WHO HEARD THE MUSIC

PIXIE POINT BAY BOOK 7

EMMA BELMONT

EMMA ONLINE

Emma loves hearing from her readers!

You can contact her at the links below.

Website: emmabelmont.com

Newsletter: emmabelmont.com/newsletter

Thanks!

1

If Maris Seaver hadn't known she was standing in the Towne Plaza of Pixie Point Bay, she'd never have recognized it. The normally tranquil scene and a throwback to a bygone era had transformed into a bustling maelstrom of activity. Excitement buzzed in the air like cicadas in summer.

"It's amazing, isn't it?" said a familiar voice.

Maris had parked in front of the Main Street Market, but it wasn't Howard that greeted her. It was Helen Tellur, a member of the crochet club, By Hook or Crook. It was located next to the general store and looked out on the Towne Plaza—and its members had to be thrilled. There was no end to the action or people that the busiest busy-bodies in the world could watch. Helen's horn-rimmed glasses framed dark blue eyes that seemed to dance with delight.

Maris smiled at the tall, elderly woman. "It's a bit on the crazy side."

Helen grinned as she nodded. "Have you ever been to one of these?"

Maris shook her head. "It was after my time." She glanced at the poster in the window of the market, the same one she had on display at the B&B. "The Fifth Annual Blues on the Bay Music Festival." Though she'd visited her aunt as a youngster, her adult work had taken her far away. It'd been years since she'd been back. She regarded Helen. "Are you a blues fan?"

"Oh, definitely," Helen said. As the elderly woman gazed at the plaza, Maris noted the large canvas tote bag she carried. Her latest doily projects were likely inside. "I mean, even if you weren't, how could you not like this?" Helen peered at her. "Are you?"

Maris smirked a little. "Only by association. Aunt Glenda was the real fan."

In the parlor at the B&B, an old Victrola was accompanied by Glenda's vast collection of blues albums. Her aunt had played them for her while they'd amused themselves with board and card games or dabbled with the Ouija board.

"Your aunt was instrumental in getting the festival started," Helen said.

Maris stared at her. "I didn't know that."

She turned back to the plaza, where a sound system was being installed in the red Oriental gazebo, and a second stage was being built at the far end. Large tents sheltered booths where food and drinks would be sold, as well as t-shirts, trinkets, and music. There were even tables where the musicians would sign autographs. It was a massive undertaking—one for which she had a new appreciation.

Helen nodded her gray head. "Yes, she was quite the driving force, your aunt."

Maris had to smile at the thought. "She was that." It was actually a trait they shared.

Helen glanced at the crochet club. "Millicent is on the festival committee, so naturally we've been privy to some of the goings on." When she turned her gaze back to Maris, she arched her eyebrows. "Perhaps next year we can look to the younger generation for some organizational help. Maybe even, shall we say, carry on a family tradition."

Maris knew she was being buttonholed, but the fact that Glenda had been involved with the start of the festival really did put it in a new light. Of course she had her hands full at the B&B during the festivities, but perhaps in the weeks leading up to it, she could find time to help.

"Who is the committee head?" Maris inquired.

Helen grinned at her. "A new one is elected every year. You just have to put your hat in the ring. This year it was Aurora Puddlefoot." She nodded to herself. "Marvelous with management."

Maris thought back to visiting the proprietor of the largest store on the plaza. Three stories tall, with everything from souvenirs to clothing and furniture, Magical Finds had at least a dozen employees.

"Yes," Maris said, "I could see that."

"Well," the older woman said, "I won't delay you any longer." She turned to go, but paused. "Unless, of course, you were stopping in for some crocheting."

"Unfortunately not," Maris said. She indicated the market as she repositioned the purse on her shoulder. "I've got a bit of shopping to do."

"Yes," Helen said, nodding. "I'm sure we're all quite busy right now." A smile lit up her face. "Good day to you."

"Have a good one," Maris replied.

THE MARKET WAS BUSIER than usual too. Shoppers, mostly tourists, were everywhere. As she took her cart up and down the aisles, Maris even noticed that Howard had hired on some new help. Young people were busily stocking shelves and answering questions from the customers. But luckily, by the time she was finished gathering everything that the B&B needed, the front counter was empty and the retired physics professor and owner of the market waved her over.

"Good morning, Maris," he said, his smile lifting his white mustache and deepening the crow's feet at the corners of his dark eyes. Though he still bore an uncanny resemblance to Einstein, his hair was neatly brushed today and his mustache combed and trimmed.

"Good morning, Howard," she said, as she unloaded the boxed goods first. "I've never seen the store so busy."

"I have," he said, quickly ringing up the goods. He gave her a wink. "This time last year."

Maris chuckled. "Well, I can see that you're prepared." One of the new employees rolled a bucket and mop past them. "The extra help is a great idea."

As Howard bagged the groceries, he said, "It's a necessity." He indicated her basket as she unloaded the vegetables. "The B&B must be full."

"Absolutely," she said. "This week's been booked for months. At first I had no idea what was going on." She laughed a little. "I told Cookie it must be a new holiday that I don't know about. She clued me in. In a way, a new holiday is exactly what it seems like." Suddenly she remembered the one item she hadn't found. "Oh, I almost forgot. I couldn't find any scrub sponges. Are you out?"

He was putting a loaded bag into the cart, but paused to look at her. "No scrubbies?" He set the bag down, and held up one finger. "Let me just check in the back." He zipped over to the door behind the counter, and disappeared.

As soon as it closed, Maris heard the usual sounds of rummaging that accompanied one of her requests. At first it sounded like boxes dragging along the ground. But then there was a bump, as though something had fallen against the door. Grunting then ensued, along with more scraping sounds and a few more bumps. But Maris didn't worry. Not only was this the time-honored process, but Howard always came up with the goods, no matter how obscure. She bagged the rest of the groceries and put everything in the cart.

But when Howard finally emerged, Maris had to stare at him in surprise. Not only was his hair going in every direction, he was sweating and breathing hard. His shocked expression and empty hands said it all.

"It's missing," he gasped. "It's gone."

Maris cocked her head at him. "The scrub sponges?" To say she was shocked was an understatement. He'd never let her down. But he obviously had a lot to deal with and she didn't want to add to the pressure. She held up a hand. "No problem. They're not a–"

"No," he whispered harshly, stumbling back to her, "not the scrubbies." He put both hands on the counter and leaned forward. "My crystal ball."

Maris couldn't help but gape at him. She'd suspected that the older man might be one of the magick folk, but she'd never imagined him reading a crystal ball. He must have realized she was staring at him.

"I know," he said. "I am a physicist, after all, but..." He shrugged his shoulders. "It's hard to argue with the results—such as they are."

Maris closed her mouth and did her best to stop gawking. He'd just confided to her that he was a crystal ball reader, a clairvoyant. Although etiquette dictated that one never asked about magic abilities, she and Cookie had managed to ferret some out. It was the unspoken rule that it was never discussed in public, so Maris took it as a measure of how upset he must be. She paused for a moment. What he'd said was curious. She glanced over her shoulder and dropped her voice.

"When you say, 'the results, such as they are', is that important?"

He glanced around as well and leaned forward. "It's cracked." He wiped a hand down his face. "Years ago, I dropped it." He shrugged again. "But what can you do? It's not like I could just get rid of it."

"Right," Maris said slowly, not sure why one wouldn't get rid of a crystal ball.

His pained expression returned. "And now it's just...just *gone*."

"Are you sure though?" she asked. "Maybe it's just–"

"I'm absolutely positive," he said. "I never move it, not since... Well, you know."

Maris glanced at the closed door behind the counter. She could only imagine the jumble of goods and supplies in there. "Would you like me to have a look? Maybe I'll be able to–"

Howard quickly shook his head, causing his tousled white hair to shudder. "No." But then he paused, as a tentative look came over his face. "But maybe you could use that, shall we say, 'sleuthing' ability of yours and find out where it's gone."

Sleuthing ability, Maris thought. Apparently Howard had his suspicions too.

She smiled a little as she nodded. "I can do that." She dug in her purse and produced a credit card from her wallet. As he rang up the bill, she put the last bag in her cart. She signed the screen on the digital tablet, and put away her card. Howard ran his hand down his face again and simply stood there looking forlorn. "I'll let you know what I find." He finally looked up at her. "I promise." She put the last bag in her cart and glanced at the door. "So I take it there are no scrubby sponges."

His face fell. "No. I'm sorry, not without…" Another shopper rolled their cart into line a few feet away. "Without the you know what."

"Ah," Maris said, wondering if the rummaging and the fractured crystal ball were related.

She'd been about to leave, when he dashed along the long wood counter and quickly retrieved one of the root beer candies that were her favorite. He handed her the brown and beige spiral stick in a tissue paper.

"A barber pole for the little lady," he said. Though he tried to smile, it was a bit lopsided. It made her appreciate their little ritual even more.

"Thank you, Howard," she said, taking it. She fixed him with an earnest gaze. "I'll be in touch."

2

B efore heading home, Maris crossed the plaza to Delia's Smokehouse to pick up her to-go order. As she passed the red gazebo, she could see the dozens of cables that had been laid and how they snaked every which way. Large speakers flanked the oriental structure, pointing toward her, while the interior held microphone stands and low speakers at foot level facing inward. Most of the cables from the equipment led to a large desk-like station with a dizzying array of knobs, slide controls, and digital readouts. A man who wore headphones was adjusting them with both hands, while a woman on the stage went from mic to mic saying 'test, test.'

Two men crossed her path carrying

folding tables, both heading toward the collection of booths. A woman with a clipboard seemed as though she was organizing a group of people who were carrying tablecloths and display stands.

Maris had to smile to herself. Aunt Glenda would have been so pleased. Not only would she have enjoyed the music, the whole town seemed to be involved. It generated business for everyone concerned, and the quiet little Victorian plaza was simply coming to life. Though she didn't know how she could help, it might be fun to get involved with the next festival.

But as she neared the smokehouse, thoughts of music, gazebos, and booths wafted away, replaced by the restaurant's delicious aromas. Smoky and spicy, with a hint of the seafood for which the region was famed, the fragrances were positively mouthwatering. The wood siding exterior had several large windows that revealed quite a multitude inside. Though Maris hadn't planned for it being so crowded, she was glad that she'd ordered ahead.

Inside it seemed that every seat was taken and there were even a few people waiting.

Nevertheless, Eugene Burnside spotted her entering and quickly came over. Despite being in his seventies, with hair and mustache a pure white, he moved his short and portly frame around like a much younger man.

"Maris Seaver," he said, smiling at her. His eyes turned into hazel-colored half-moons. "Good to see you. It feels like a month of Sundays."

"It does indeed," she agreed. Getting the B&B ready to be fully occupied had taken a bit of time, not to mention work. "How have you been?"

"Superb," he said. "Couldn't ask for more. Business is jumping, Delia is cooking up a storm, and the festival starts tomorrow. It just doesn't get any better."

Coming from anyone else, Maris would have suspected hyperbole. But Eugene was different. It wasn't his restaurant work or the fact that his daughter had taken over the place that kept him young—it was his attitude. He had to be the most positive person she'd ever met.

She smiled back at him, and indicated the packed room. "I'll bet even Delia is having a hard time keeping up with this." She noticed that, like Howard, they'd hired some extra help. One young man was bussing tables, and there seemed to be a new waitress as well.

He shook his head and grinned. "There's no stopping that girl of mine, but I'm afraid she won't have time to come out and say hi." He went to a small table at the end of the waiting area and picked up one of the white paper bags that had been stapled closed at the top. Under the staple was her name and the bill. "Four Shrimp Po' Boys?"

"That would be mine," she said, reaching into her purse for her wallet.

Eugene set the order on the hostess podium as a young couple passed him on the way out. "Thanks folks," he called out to them. "Keep your pepper dry."

Although the man grinned and waved at him, the young woman looked vaguely puzzled. Maris hid her smile as she brought out the wallet.

Eugene reached under the podium, frowned, and then crouched down to look underneath it. "That's odd." He stood and looked at the table with the to-go orders. "Where'd it go?"

Maris took out her credit card. "Where did what go?"

Eugene scratched his head. "The credit card reader."

The waitress passed them and went to the small group that was waiting. "I can seat you now."

They followed her from the waiting area, while Eugene moved the white bags and looked behind them. For a moment, as Maris watched the diners wending their way through the packed diner, she wondered if some extra staff at the B&B might help next year.

Eugene went back to the podium, and looked behind it again. "I always leave it here." Then he glanced back at the table, as a young family came in. He smiled at them. "I'll be right with you folks." He fetched a few menus and handed them out. "It'll just be a few minutes."

When he returned, Maris asked, "Would cash be quicker?" as yet another group came in.

"I'll be right with you folks," he said, smiling and passing out more menus.

Maris took out some cash.

"Oh, the cash," Eugene said, and looked around him. Only then did Maris realize there was no cash register.

Eugene glanced at her, thought for a second, and shook his head. He picked up her order and handed it to her. "I'll put it on your tab," he said, then added, "If you don't mind that is."

As an older couple exited, the man said, "Best crab salad I've ever had. Please give our compliments to the chef."

"Thank you, sir, I'll do just that," Eugene said, beaming at him. "Keep your pepper dry, and we'll keep our cookers smoking."

Maris put away her wallet. "I'll catch up with you later, Eugene. I can see you're busy. Do put it on my tab."

He gave her a grateful look. "Thank you, Maris." As she headed to the door, he called out after her, "Keep your pepper dry."

She smiled and gave him a quick wave, and then exited to the sidewalk.

"Phew," she exhaled.

If she and Cookie thought they were busy, Delia's Smokehouse was setting a new standard. Despite the new employees, Eugene was going to be exhausted at the end of the day.

But as Maris headed back to her car across the busy plaza, she realized two things: the disappearance of the credit card reader was the second missing item in as many visits, and she didn't have a tab.

3

I n the shade of the side porch of the B&B, Maris, Cookie, and Bear settled down for their lunch. Although the B&B's diminutive chef and their outsized handyman would typically be working in the garden on such a beautiful day, it was all hands on deck when the lightkeeper's house was full to capacity. Even so, they always made time for lunch. As usual, Maris placed two of the sandwiches in front of Bear, leaving one each for her and Cookie. The fresh lemonade had already been poured.

"Thank you, Maris," he said, staring at the wrapped subs.

As usual, their handyman's full beard was as nicely trimmed as his dark, short cropped hair. The white t-shirt, under the blue bib apron of his overalls, was clean and stretched just a bit over his burgeoning middle. With a delicate touch that belied the big hands, he carefully began to unwrap his first sandwich.

"You're welcome, Bear," she replied.

His face lit up when he saw what was inside. "Po' Boys."

"Really?" Cookie said, unwrapping hers as Maris did the same.

Ruth "Cookie" Calderon was a spry and petite seventy-year old. Aunt Glenda's best friend, she'd been living and cooking at the B&B for decades. Her salt and pepper hair—though mostly salt now—fell straight and was shoulder length. As she regarded her sandwich, her dark eyes glimmered. She looked down at her food with a critical eye that made Maris pause.

"This must be a new menu item," the chef said.

Though Bear had picked up his sandwich and was poised to take a bite, he paused as well.

"It is," Maris said, watching the diminutive woman turn the opened wrapper, slowly spinning the sandwich in place.

"Good presentation," Cookie said.

Barbecued jumbo shrimp with a nice helping of smoky sauce was cradled on pillowy soft New Orleans-style French rolls with paper thin crusts. Thin-sliced heirloom tomatoes were layered on the shrimp, and Delia's house slaw topped the tomatoes.

The chef picked it up. "Very fresh bread," she said nodding. "More important to a sandwich than most people realize. But the real test?"

She took a bite—not from the end and not from the middle, but somewhere in-between.

Maris exchanged a look with Bear, as Cookie slowly chewed.

Suddenly Cookie bobbed her head, and made the "Mmmm" sound that signaled something delicious. She set the sandwich down and gave them an emphatic okay sign.

Bear immediately took a bite, but Maris took a moment to breathe a little sigh of relief. She'd never known Delia or Eugene to serve anything but the freshest and best. But even they might be able to take a misstep with a new item. It was odd how the individual ingredients in a dish could be excellent, and yet the combination was off. As she took her first bite though, Maris knew they had another winner on their hands.

The bread was so soft as to be almost non-existent. Instead, it was the taste of the crispy shrimp that really came through. A touch of spice from the thick sauce, along with the smoke of the BBQ, helped to highlight the seafood. The cool and sweet tomato was a great compliment. But finally, it was the house slaw that provided that slight bit of crunchy texture that filled the mouth perfectly. Maris couldn't help but bob her head too. The cole slaw was great on its own—a vibrant combination of green and red cabbage with shredded carrots, all enveloped in just a thin coating of dressing—but on the sandwich it was genius.

"Do you taste the Dijon mustard and celery seed in the slaw?" Cookie asked, smiling. "Very inventive."

Maris covered her mouth with one hand. "I'd never have thought of putting shrimp in a sandwich."

Bear wiped his mouth and beard with a napkin. "Very good," he declared quickly, before taking another bite.

For some moments, the three of them

simply enjoyed their food outside in the glorious weather. Brilliant sunshine rained down on Cookie's herb garden, and poured into the greenhouse beyond it. A light briny breeze from the bay gently stirred the plants as well as providing some relief from the midday heat.

"What are you working on today, Bear?" Cookie asked.

He was just opening his second sandwich and, for a moment, Maris wondered if she shouldn't have got him three. His fingers paused, and he looked at the chef. "Time to take care of the Old Girl's optic house." When he looked to the top of the lighthouse, Cookie and Maris did the same. "I need to pack some grease into the ball bearings."

Maris looked at him. "Ball bearings?"

"The mechanism that turns the fresnel lens," he said, and made a small circling motion with his finger. "At the center of the base are the ball bearings that allow it to spin."

Of course, Maris thought. It'd never occurred to her what it actually took to make the beam turn. As she continued to gaze up at it, she wondered what else she didn't know about the Old Girl.

"You have to grease it?" Cookie asked, sandwich in hand.

Bear nodded his big head. "It's not sealed." He paused and, when there seemed to be no more questions, he dug into his next sandwich.

With still half of her sandwich remaining, Cookie put it down and wrapped it back up. "This will be good later."

Though Maris could easily have eaten the whole thing, she did as the thinner and healthier chef did—though with some disappointment.

"How was town?" the chef asked, as she picked up her lemonade.

"Incredibly busy," Maris said, wrapping the Po' Boy. "And a little strange."

"Oh?" Cookie said. "The busy I understand, since it's festival time. But the strange?"

Maris recounted the two missing objects from the two different owners.

Cookie smirked a little. "A crystal ball, eh?" She nodded. "I'd have put him down as an astrologer with all his knowledge of the stars and such. Very interesting."

"But someone stole it?" Bear asked.

He'd finished both his sandwiches and

had been sitting back, but now leaned forward.

Maris nodded. "According to Howard, it's always in the same spot and now it's nowhere to be found."

"Same with Eugene's credit card reader?" Cookie asked.

"Yep," Maris replied. "It's always behind the hostess podium." She picked up her lemonade. "I've seen him take it from there a dozen times at least." She took a tart sip. "So that makes two."

"Three," Bear said. Maris and Cookie both whipped their heads around to stare at him. "My honey."

"Oh no," Cookie exclaimed. "From the hive?"

Bear shook his head quickly. "No. The bees wouldn't permit it. I'm the only one allowed." He gazed down at the deck. "I had a jar in my truck." He ducked his head sheepishly. "I was bringing it to you."

"Well," Maris said, "thank you anyway. But you say you put it in your truck and it disappeared?"

"After I stopped for gas at Flour Power," he said. "I thought that if someone was really hungry enough to take it, they could have it. That was fine. The bees make a lot, so I can bring more tomorrow."

Maris had to smile at the big softy.

"That was this morning?" Cookie asked him.

Bear nodded. "I went inside to pay my bill. When I came back it was gone."

"Do you know what time?" Maris asked.

Bear slowly combed his fingers through his beard. "Close to eight o'clock."

"Were there any strangers there?" Maris asked. "Anyone you didn't recognize?"

He nodded. "Lots. It's festival time. Fabiola and Jude were both busy."

Flour Power Sandwiches & Gas was part filling station, part sandwich shop, and part auto repair. The young couple from Haiti were likely experiencing their first festival as well.

"Hmm," Maris said, thinking back to the plaza. "I was at the market about three hours after you were at the station. Then I picked up the sandwiches about half past noon."

"Plenty of time to make it from one spot to the next," the chef concluded. She scooted back her chair. "Well, I've got to go move that laundry to the dryer." She picked up her sandwich and turned to Maris. "Thanks for picking up lunch. That was fantastic."

Bear stood as well. "Thank you, Maris. It was delicious." He finished off his glass of juice with an appreciative "Ah." Cookie took his glass along with hers. "Thank you, Cookie." He looked at Maris as she stood too. "Time for the bearings."

Maris picked up her sandwich and empty glass. "Thanks, Bear. For me, I think it's time for some cleaning."

4

———

As Maris followed Cookie into the house, one of the guests was just coming down the steps.

"Good timing," Bowdie Johnson said.

Maris paused in the hallway, smiling. "Bowdie," she said. "Timing is everything, they say."

"In music and life," the young man agreed.

Maris had already learned that the blues guitarist's name was a sort of shortening of his real name: Beau de Glen Johnson. He was a young looking forty, with light brown hair, a stubble mustache, and steel blue eyes. Painfully thin, his oversized bling made him look even thinner. From the various festival posters, she also knew that he was one of the headliners. Like the other musicians, he'd arrived ahead of the start of the festival.

"Is there something I can do for you?" she asked.

He nodded at her sandwich leftovers. "I'm just about to head off and forage for lunch. I was wondering if you could give me a recommendation."

"I'd be delighted," she said, and hefted the sandwich. "And I can start with a whole hearted recommendation for Delia's Smokehouse, specializing in all manner of barbecue, not to mention some sizzling sauces. We just enjoyed their BBQ Shrimp Po' Boy sandwich. Truly excellent."

"Smells great," he agreed.

"I have some menus for Delia's," she said. "And, if BBQ and spice aren't your thing, but sandwiches are, there's Flour Power Sandwiches & Gas just outside of town. Excellent fresh coffee and pastries there too." She gazed out the library's large window toward the bay. "But if you have a little time and would appreciate something a bit more upscale, then I can recommend Plateau 7. You'll need a reservation, but the French cuisine and the amazing view simply cannot be beat."

He considered for a moment, and stuck his hands into the pockets of his black, skinny-fit jeans. "I think I'll try the place on the bay."

Maris smiled and nodded. "A great choice. Let me get one of their cards for you." She went to the dining room, fetched an elegant and simple business card from a drawer of the sideboard, and brought it back. Bowdie had moved into the library and was looking out the window.

"I can't believe how clear it is," he said, "after that thick fog this morning."

"Every morning," she said, pausing to look out as well.

"Every morning?" he said. Then he glanced in the direction of the lighthouse. "I guess that's why you need the beacon."

"Exactly," Maris said, handing him the business card. "It's hard to make out the restaurant from here." She pointed in its direction. "But you can definitely see the lighthouse from there."

He looked up the coast and then gazed down at the card. "Super, thanks."

As he tucked it into his back pocket, she said, "Will you have time on your visit to see any of the sights? We have kayaks and paddleboards at the dock below the lighthouse."

He pursed his lips and slowly shook his head. "I'm not really one for sports. I had to give all that up when I was a kid." He raised his hands and wriggled his fingers slightly. "I have to protect my hands."

Maris nodded, slightly embarrassed. "Oh, of course. That should have occurred to me. Your hands are your living."

"I couldn't have said it better," he agreed. "But really, when I was young, there was no time. It was guitar, morning, noon, and night—mostly night." He smiled a little. "While the other guys were shooting hoops or playing video games, I was sneaking into bars to hear the bands."

Since he still looked like a gangly teenager, Maris could almost picture it. "So, not exactly a conventional childhood."

Bowdie laughed. "It is if you play the blues. I even took up smoking to roughen up my voice, trying to sound and look older." Maris's eyebrows flew up, and he held up his hand. "But I've stopped. That was definitely not the smartest move of my life—plus it didn't work. I've been thrown out of more bars than I can count." He rubbed his stubble. "Until the facial hair. That was a life saver."

Bowdie had a baritone quality to his voice. Not as rumbling and low as a deep bass, but still very pleasant. Maris couldn't imagine actually trying to mar it.

Just then, the musician's stomach rumbled, and he covered it with both hands. He laughed a little. "But man does not live on a steady diet of the blues alone. I guess I better get a move on. Thanks for the tips."

She watched as he headed to the front door, before turning toward the kitchen. He was right—the Po' Boy leftovers did smell good. She'd better put them away before she finished them.

5

As the late afternoon sun slanted through the B&B's many gabled windows, the day's chores were just coming under control. Maris and Cookie had spent almost the entire day with all their usual tasks. While the chef saw to her kitchen and the bathrooms, Maris took care of turning down the beds, dusting, and vacuuming. Cookie washed the sheets and towels, and Maris folded and put everything away. As she took out the trash, Cookie made sure that enough toiletries and healthy snacks were on hand. Occasionally the phone would ring for a reservation, but mostly they bustled back and forth.

Downstairs in the hallway, Cookie had paused outside the kitchen, and caught

Maris's eye as she left the library. The chef put her hands on her hips. "I'd say we've earned a nice cup of tea."

"If not the Good Housekeeping Seal of Approval," Maris agreed. "Let me just put away this duster."

Cookie chuckled. "I'll put the water on the boil."

But as they started for the kitchen, a tiny, tinny harmonica-like meow stopped them.

"Mojo," Maris said. "Where have you been?"

More than likely her slightly pudgy and entirely fluffy little black cat had been taking his usual nap in their room. His big orange eyes stared up at her and, in answer, he gave her another meow, sounding a bit insistent now.

"I think you're being paged," the chef said.

Although Maris went over to give him a pet, he didn't wait for her. Instead he quickly turned and bounced into the parlor.

"Bait and switch," Cookie said, but the two of them followed him in.

There, he lightly leapt up to the coffee table and sat next to the Ouija board.

"Oh, thank goodness," Maris said lowly.

Cookie came to her side. "Do you think this has to do with the thefts?" she whispered.

Maris shrugged a little. "I don't know," she said quietly, "but I sure hope so."

As they fell silent, Mojo seemed to settle in, his eyes focused on some unseen place in the distance. His tail went still and his whiskers froze in place, while all the energy of his little body seemed to be channeled into his ears. The downy triangles went into overdrive, spinning one way and then the other, as though his "voices of the spirits" radar was homing in on something only he could hear.

Maris and Cookie exchanged a look. As many times as Maris had seen this, she could still hardly believe it was happening. Neither she nor the chef doubted Mojo's ability any longer. But if she was going to take advantage of these sessions, she would need to seriously up her interpretive ability when it came to solving crimes. Maybe it was the nature of the Ouija in the first place, the way the board doled out a clue of several letters at most. But she was determined to figure it out.

Slowly, Mojo's paw moved to the heart-shaped planchette, and Maris and Cookie both leaned forward a bit. He pushed it steadily until it came to a brief rest over the first letter: F. Maris immediately started to imagine names that started with F. Fabiola Toussaint? She and her husband owned and operated Flour Power. But as the planchette moved on, it traveled just a short distance to the "I".

Well, it's not Fabiola, Maris thought. Not that she could have imagined the gorgeous woman as a thief. Nor were there any other people in Pixie Point Bay whose names, first or last, started with the letters F and I.

As she and Cookie stared at the board, Mojo's paw seemed to twitch and the clear lens of the planchette centered itself directly over the "V". Then it was just a short distance back up to the first row, ending on the "E".

"Five?" Cookie whispered.

Maris had to shake her head. Of all the vague clues that Mojo had spelled out, this had to be the worst.

Five.

It could be part of an address, a phone number, the number of people in a family, the number of countries they'd recently vis-ited. It could be anything.

"Good grief," Maris muttered.

She began to turn away when Cookie put a hand on her arm. "There's more."

Maris stared at the chef. There was never any more, no matter how many times she'd asked the little cat. But as she turned to look at the board, she had to watch in disbelief. Mojo was spelling something else.

As she cocked her head at the transfixed cat, the planchette went again to the "F".

"Here we go again," Cookie said under her breath.

But it wasn't a repeat of the first word. In-stead, Mojo had to stretch his leg almost all the way to the far side of the board—where the planchette stopped over the "O".

Five for, Maris thought. *Or maybe five fobs.*

But the next letter, all the way across the board again, ended more speculation: L.

She and Cookie exchanged another look. Mojo had them stumped.

But as they watched, he slowly scooted the planchette back toward the middle of the board. It stuttered a little, as though it had caught on something—maybe the seam of the fold—and Maris found herself holding her breath. Finally though, it resumed its course and came to a stop on the "D".

"Five fold?" Cookie whispered, just as Mojo sat back. With a blink of his big orange eyes, he stood and shook out his fur. Then he gave them one of his signature meows.

Maris smiled at the little creature. As she gently rubbed the soft fur on the top of his head, he nudged upward for a scratch behind the ears. "You've earned it," she told him.

"Five fold," Cookie said, frowning. She picked up the planchette and turned it over in her hands before looking up at Maris. "Do you have any idea what that means?"

Maris shook her head, as she picked up the fluffy cat, who immediately purred. "I was going to ask you the same thing."

"It almost makes me want to check the laundry and see if it's folded," the chef said.

"Or if any of it is missing," Maris suggested.

Without another word, they went to the linen closet in the utility room, at the extreme opposite end of the house. Cookie threw the cabinet doors open, but a quick check revealed that everything seemed to be in place. She patted each of the neat piles as she counted them off.

The chef shrugged. "Of course I'm not sure what missing sheets would have told us anyway." She backed up a pace. "Now I really think it's time for tea." She closed the doors, gave Mojo a pet, and headed toward the kitchen.

Maris turned, giving the little black cat a long stroke. "And a snack for you, young man. I don't know what you're trying to tell us, but it's appreciated all the same."

He gave her a plaintive little mew as they followed Cookie down the hall.

6

Maris had barely had enough time to finish her tea, when it was time to start preparations for the Wine Down. She was going to need extra time this evening, since she was breaking with tradition. But it had always been something that she'd wanted to try, or rather revive: a fondue.

Some weeks ago she'd found the vintage copper fondue set tucked away in a low kitchen cupboard. She'd cleaned and polished it, along with the matching forks, and this evening was as good a time as any to give it a spin. Unlike modern electric models, it was heated with a can of gel fuel.

With the flame lit and warming the pot, Maris fetched the ingredients. For the fondue, she gathered the fresh cheeses from the dairy in Cheeseman Village: Fontina, Gouda, and Gruyere. As the cubes melted, she added the secret sauce ingredients that elevated this fondue from melted cheese to a luxurious taste experience. Sauvignon Blanc formed the base of the liquid ingredients, accompanied by a shot of brandy, a splash of lemon juice, and a dollop of Dijon mustard. Finally, cornstarch returned some of the thickness, and nutmeg finished off the flavor profile.

As the pot simmered, Maris assembled the dippers: boiled new baby potatoes, which she'd allowed to cool, steamed broccoli and cauliflower florets, asparagus, button mushrooms, cherry tomatoes, and cubes of Cookie's sourdough bread. As she laid them all out, she had to admit it was a beautiful spread, even if she did say so herself. The colorful vegetables might be something she'd add to the regular cheeseboard.

With the food set, she opened the wines she'd selected. The dry Prosecco would be able to cut through the cheese, while the Syrah, also dry but red, would do the same. A carafe of cranberry juice and a plate of oatmeal cookies, made sure even the kids could participate.

"Wow," Bowdie said, from the door. "I thought the B&B didn't provide dinner."

Maris grinned at him, as she put down the last of the wine glasses. "Let's just call it a blast from the past."

He was too young to remember the fondue parties of the 70s, but her Aunt Glenda had shown Maris how it was done. On more than one occasion, she and Cookie and Maris had sat around the pot in the kitchen. They'd even let her light the flame and take charge of the melt.

Before she could ask Bowdie how lunch at Plateau 7 had been, the McGrath boys made a beeline for the cookies, running around the musician.

"*Boys*," their mother said. "We're going to dinner."

Tami and Jim McGrath, though staying at the B&B during the festival, had come for the outdoor activities. The family spent almost no time at the B&B, so Maris had hardly seen them, but they were all a matched set. All four had coppery red hair in different lengths and cuts, as well as freckles.

"One each," Jim McGrath said, coming up behind them. He nodded to Bowdie. "Sorry about that."

The musician only laughed. "I know better than to stand between a hungry boy and his cookie."

As the older McGraths herded the boys out of the room, Maris and Bowdie were joined by Spats Thackery.

"Oh," said the blues drummer, and another player in the festival. He clasped his hands in front of his chest. "Now this is what I call Wine and Cheese."

Maris smiled at the older man. He was completely bald and his dark skin was the tiniest bit shiny on the dome of his nicely shaped head. He wore a goatee that had yet to show any gray, but his hands showed his age—slightly gnarled though immaculately groomed. And true to his name, he wore white cloth spats over his patent black shoes. He was dressed in a dark plaid suit and vest, but no tie.

"Spats Thackery," Maris said, nodding to him. "May I introduce Bowdie Johnson."

The drummer beamed at the guitarist. "No intros needed." He stuck out his hand to the younger man. "Been a fan for some time now."

"High praise indeed," Bowdie said, grasping the man's hand. "From the drummer who backed Spitfire Shaw for what —twelve years? Man, that gig in Monterey..."

As the two musicians fell into deep and detailed music conversation, Maris poured the wine, a glass of white and a glass of red, offering both to Bowdie, who took the white. Though she'd intended to pour another, so Spats could have his choice, he reached out for the red.

"Not so fast, young lady," he said taking it. "I'm not particularly picky." He grinned at Bowdie. "Shall we check out that amazing spread?"

"Please," Maris said, extending her hand. "I hope you enjoy."

As the two men picked up plates, fondue forks, and dippers, the final two guests of the B&B arrived. George Brunell was a heavy-set man. Darker skinned than Spats and about the same age, his hair had definitely begun to turn white. Maris's brief chat with him when he'd arrived had told her that he was retired and here for the blues festival.

Megan Kantor trailed just behind him. In her mid-fifties with flaming red hair and a hawkish look to her narrow face, she was a journalist covering the festival for a travel magazine. Known for her Pulitzer award winning work—a mention of which she managed to work into their first conversation—her sharp eyes seemed to see everything.

Maris welcomed them and offered to pour wine. After all the introductions were done, Maris poured herself a glass of the Syrah. As everyone dipped and sipped, conversation naturally turned to the blues festival. It seemed as though George was a living encyclopedia about blues music, often filling in facts and dates that the two musicians were unsure about.

"Nope," he was saying. "You're talking about the third album they released. 1965."

Spats thought for a moment and then snapped his fingers. "You're right." He regarded the big man. "Again."

Megan hung back, preferring to sit at the table and take notes. From time to time, she sipped her Prosecco and turned her watchful gaze on each of the other guests in turn. Mostly though, she scribbled in the medium sized journal that had an elastic band to keep it closed. Her writing was tiny.

For a moment, Maris thought back to Mojo's clue: five fold. Right now in the dining room, there were five people, including herself. But if she were involved with the thefts, wouldn't she know?

Bowdie turned to her. "Are you a blues fan, Maris?"

"I'm learning," she said, honestly, prompting a bit of laughter. She used her wine glass to indicate the parlor room at the front of the house. "It was my aunt who created the collection of albums."

"Oh, I saw that," George said, with something like wonder in his deep voice. "Amazing collection." He glanced at the guitarist and the drummer. "Well worth a look, and maybe even a listen." He turned back to Maris. "Does the old Victrola work?"

Maris nodded. "It does. Glenda never kept antiques just for the sake of show."

"So I take it you won't be attending the festival?" Bowdie said.

Maris finished sipping her wine. "Oh no. I'll be there. I wouldn't miss it. I may not be an aficionado, but I have a friend who most definitely is. We'll be attending the festival together."

Spats lifted his glass to her. "Well however you can get there, young lady," he gave her a wink, "I say get there." He indicated the sideboard. "And before we dive back into the fondue pot, may I thank you for the good eats."

"Here, here," the other men chimed in.

George patted his stomach. "It was a meal."

Maris beamed back at them. If the Wine Down was meant to do anything, it was exactly this—friendly conversation in a relaxed and welcoming setting. The evening had been perfect.

She lifted her glass in return. "To the hottest music in a blues festival ever. I honestly can't wait."

7

———

The next day, after the B&B's chores were done—and Maris had changed her outfit three times—she was ready. The cream-colored, short-sleeved shirt flared at the bottom, and she used one of Aunt Glenda's silver-trimmed belts to bring it in at the waist. She smiled at the nice slimming effect it had. The blouse extended over the top of her aqua blue skirt, which swished dramatically when she turned. A turquoise necklace and matching open-toed heels finished off the outfit.

She turned to the bed, where Mojo was lounging, sprawled on his side. "What do you think?" He raised his head, his sleepy orange eyes gazing dreamily at her. "Better?"

In answer, he rolled to his back, stretched his front legs up and over his head, then let them slowly fall to the comforter.

She smiled as she walked over and gave his soft belly a gentle rub. "I'll take that as a double high five." He only sighed in return.

As she gave herself one more quick check in the mirror, she adjusted the necklace. Though it wasn't enough to highlight her blue eyes, the cream shirt was a good compliment to her curly, strawberry blond hair. She picked up her purse from the dressing table and quietly left the room.

She was halfway down the hall, when there was a knock at the front door. Since guests came and went at all hours of the day and night, Maris knew that had to be Mac. Though he could have simply come in, Maris had noted on previous occasions that he never did. He always knocked and waited for someone to answer. Initially she'd thought it might be some sort of police officer protocol, since his first visits had been on official business. But now she simply chalked it up to politeness. She could already see him through the front door's beveled glass panels. He was smiling.

As she opened it, she said, "Good afternoon, Mac."

His smile grew wider. "Good afternoon."

Easily six feet tall and athletically built, Sheriff Daniel "Mac" McKenna was the most eligible bachelor in Medio County. His cool gray eyes were kind, and almost matched his salt and pepper hair. But it was his easy manner and sense of calm that Maris found most attractive. Of course, it didn't hurt that he was handsome.

"I don't think I've seen this outfit before," he said. "Very nice."

He was dressed in light khaki slacks and a powder blue polo shirt. "We're almost twinsies," she said. "But in reverse." She was just about to close the door when she remembered her phone. "Oh. Hang on just a second. I forgot my phone."

As Mac stepped inside and closed the door behind him, Maris went back to her room. Mojo was in the exact same position, paws reaching over his head for the pillow. Quietly, she went to the bedside table, unplugged her phone, and crept out. When she went back up the hallway though, she found Mac in the parlor, crouched in front of the old Victrola looking through Aunt Glenda's collection of blues LPs.

When he noticed her at the door, he said, "I'm looking for that album of Woody Howard's. I thought I'd play a little bit for you since we're going to be hearing someone today who's clearly influenced by the late great." He flipped the vertical records back and forth. "But I don't see it here." He stood. "That's a shame."

Naturally he knew the collection better than her. "Well, maybe you can just describe it to me," she suggested.

Mac rubbed his chin, still looking at the records. "It's not that. It's a shame if it's missing because, not only is it one of the best examples of Delta Blues that was ever recorded, it's a very collectible record. In fact, it's pretty valuable."

"Oh?" Maris said. It'd never occurred to her that any of Glenda's old records would have more than sentimental value. "It's probably just misplaced. In fact, I wouldn't be surprised if the guests had noticed it when they'd been looking through the collection. There was even some discussion of the albums last night at the Wine Down."

"Your guests?" Mac asked.

She nodded. "Two of the festival's per-formers are staying here, along with a retired blues fan, and a reporter covering the event. We've also got a young family, but I don't think they have an interest in the blues." She looked thoughtfully at the records, then back at him. "I'm sure it's just been misplaced," she concluded. "I'll make a search for it when I get back."

"Right," Mac said, glancing at his watch. "We should get a move on."

As they went to the front door, Maris sud-denly thought of the missing crystal ball, the jar of honey, and the credit card machine. She frowned and glanced back at the parlor.

Had one of Glenda's albums now joined their ranks?

Mac must have seen her look. "I'm sure it'll turn up. As you say, it's probably just lost in the shuffle." He opened the door for her.

For a moment she considered telling him about the other missing items, but quickly discarded the notion. She'd hardly had a chance to do any of her own snooping. At this point, discretion would likely be the better course.

"I'm sure you're right," she said, stepping through.

8
___

Though Maris didn't know much about the history of blues music, she had the feeling of being transported in time. As she and Mac stood with hundreds of other people in front of the red gazebo, they listened to Bowdie and the band backing him play a soulful rendition of a song that Maris didn't recognize. Even so, there was something irresistible about the slow beat and the repetition of the various lyrics. Bowdie's mournful lead guitar wailed and lilted, as he seemed to channel the notes right from the air. Maris wondered if the sound wasn't helped by the glass tube that he used. He wore it over one of his fingers, sliding it up and down the neck of the guitar, and using a pick with the other hand.

The crowd around them were all bobbing their heads or tapping their toes, eyes riveted on the guitar player. As Maris scanned around them, she saw Minako not too far away. Minako noticed her as well, gave her a little wave, and came over.

"Amazing," the shorter Asian woman said into Maris's ear. "Each year gets better than the last."

"I wouldn't know about previous years," Maris said, leaning toward her, "but I'd have to agree that it's pretty amazing." She regarded the owner of the bookstore. "Are you a fan?"

Minako shook her head, smiling. "Not really." She raised her phone for Maris to see. "But it's a great photo op, and I've also done some videos."

Maris recalled seeing the display of vintage photos from Pixie Point Bay's past in one of her store's front windows. Then she remembered Minako's previous career.

"It must be an archivist's dream," Maris said.

Minako eagerly nodded. "Definitely. I'm already thinking of mounting a small exhibit at Inklings. Just the festival, over the years."

"That sounds fabulous," Maris said. "I'd love to see it, since I missed the rest." No doubt there'd be pictures of Aunt Glenda. "Is Alfred minding the store?"

Minako and her husband owned Inklings New & Used Bookstore, one of the larger buildings on the plaza.

She nodded. "Getting ready for the performance there too." She glanced at her phone. "In fact, I'd better go help him. I'll see you later."

"See you later," Maris said.

As Bowdie finished, the crowd erupted in applause.

As he clapped, Mac grinned at her. "He's really in fine form today."

"He was wonderful," she agreed.

"Harmonious concert rung in every part," he said, "while simple melody pour'd moving on the heart."

She grinned at him. "So Burns appreciated music?"

Mac nodded. "Oh yes. Many of Old Rabbie's poems were made into songs. Or rather, he set his lyrics to the tunes of traditional music."

"Really," Maris said. "I had no idea he was a songwriter."

"People are still singing some of them," he said, and glanced at the stage. "Not unlike some of this blues music."

"By the way," she said, "what is that thing that Bowdie wears on his finger. It looks like the neck of a wine bottle."

"It's probably the neck of a wine bottle," he said. When she raised her eyebrows, he added, "It's called a slide. Some players like to have them custom made, but I've read that Bowdie likes to go old school."

Without a preamble, the guitarist turned to the musicians behind him, seemed to count off, and they started. This tune was a good deal faster—and she immediately liked it better. As Mac kept time with a tap on his leg, Maris bobbed her head. The high energy of the song was infectious.

"Aurora thinks it's too loud," said the storekeeper into Maris's ear.

Maris turned to find Aurora Puddlefoot, in her gypsy garb. The older woman wore her usual creative makeup—bright red lipstick and matching dots arching over her eyebrows. Her platinum hair fell in long braids, though most of it was hidden by the colorful purple hair wrap that matched her robes.

"You don't like the blues?" Maris asked, tapping her toes now.

"Aurora likes the business," she said. "But the music?" She waved her hand as though swatting a fly. "No." She eyed Mac, on the other side of Maris. "But Aurora sees that you are gaining an appreciation for the blues." The older woman gave her a wink, briefly exposing her bright orange eye makeup. "Good for you."

"I'm surprised," Maris told her. "Helen mentioned that you're this year's head of the festival's organizing committee."

The older woman nodded. "This is true. Aurora wanted to see it done right."

"Well, you've done a magnificent job."

As the owner of Magical Finds, the largest store in the town, let alone on the plaza, Maris wasn't surprised that Aurora wanted to make sure everything ran smoothly. "Business is brisk?" she asked.

Aurora nodded. "Excellent. Truly excellent." She glanced toward her three story Victorian, a former hotel. But as another song started, she covered her ears. "Aurora will go back now," she shouted, "but she saw you and wanted to say hello."

They exchanged a brief hug. "Good to see you, Aurora."

But as the storekeeper made her escape to the rear of the plaza, Maris's gaze followed her. As it did, she noted that just around the corner from Magical Finds was Delia's Smokehouse, and she couldn't help but think of the missing credit card machine. Now it seemed that her B&B might also have been the victim of a theft.

But the only people who'd been there, aside from the usual contingent, were the guests. Maris watched Bowdie finish a solo as the crowd thundered it's approval. Of all the B&B's occupants, only he, Spats, and George would have a special interest in the album. Though she hated to think that any of them would be capable of stealing it, she knew where her investigation needed to start.

9

———

Though anxious to get to the bottom of the thefts, Maris knew the investigation would have to wait. She and Mac arrived inside Inklings just as a small acoustic group was starting up on the ground floor. Spats was playing a small, single snare drum, along with two guitarists and a harmonica player.

Mac leaned close. "This is the group I was talking about earlier," he said. "A lot like the one on that album of your aunt's."

As the leader of the quartet began to sing, Maris eyed the crowd. Minako and Alfred were there, of course. Alfred was refilling the apple cider decanters that were always on hand in the bookstore. He must be doing double duty with the free drinks with so many people in the store. It looked like the bookshelves on this level had been moved away from the lobby area to make room for the low, square stage. Even so, Maris noted a number of coffee table volumes about blues music and musicians artfully placed in hard-to-miss locations. Like the other businesses in town, including hers, it looked like the bookstore was doing well too.

Behind the long counter, Maris once again admired the vertical garden on the wall behind it. Minako had cultivated succulents mixed with draping flowers, and the entire feel of it was lush and tranquil. Some of them stretched toward the large display windows at the front of the store, where sunlight poured in.

Maris also spotted George, her retired B&B guest, in one of the overstuffed chairs close to the small stage, listening intently and smiling. Another guest, journalist Megan Kantor, was also on hand—taking notes as always. Most of the crowd stood, as did she and Mac.

At the end of the song there was enthusiastic applause, and George used two fingers in his mouth to give a loud whistle. The rhythm guitarist launched right into the next song with a pounding strum that seemed familiar.

"I think I recognize this," Maris said into Mac's ear.

He grinned at her. "You should."

After the lead guitarist played a few licks, the singer stepped up to the mic and belted out the fact that he "had the key to the highway," to which most of the crowd sang along. Maris recognized it as one of Glenda's favorites and had to smile. Though she didn't know the entire song, she definitely hummed what she knew. The harmonica player took a particularly nice solo before the lead guitar took over again and finished the song. The room erupted in applause and whistles, with Maris and Mac clapping and cheering.

Three more numbers followed, enjoyed by the crowd with just as much enthusiasm as the first two. As the group signed off and left the stage, a number of fans crowded forward for autographs, with photos and pens in hand. Maris was pleased to see Spats signing a couple of CDs before he saw her and came over.

"Maris," he said, "good to see you here. Thanks for listening."

"I wouldn't have missed it," she said. "You and the band were wonderful."

The older man bent his head to her. "Much obliged." When he looked up, he noticed Mac.

"Spats Thackery," she said to him. "This is Mac McKenna."

As the two men shook, Mac said, "One of the best renditions of *Key to the Highway* I've ever heard. Just amazing."

"Thank you, sir," Spats said, smiling as the crowd dispersed around them.

"I gotta say," Mac began, "I've been listening to you since–"

"Mr. Thackery," Megan Kantor said, tapping the drummer on the shoulder. "I wonder if you'd answer some questions for a piece I'm writing."

The interruption hadn't exactly been rude, particularly given her profession. But the words 'brusque' and 'abrasive' sprang to Maris's mind.

Spats turned and smiled at the woman. "I'm sure I'd be delighted, just as long as its quick, because I'm in the middle of talking to these good folks here."

Maris smiled to herself. She hadn't been the only one to notice the journalist's butt-in attitude. But Megan wasn't deterred in the least. She briskly opened her notebook and clicked her ballpoint pen.

"How does this festival compare with the others on the circuit?" she asked, already looking at the journal.

"It's the best there is," he said. "Bar none." He nodded to himself. "And you might say I've been to a few."

"Any one that stands out in your mind as the worst?" she asked.

Spats frowned at her—or the top of her head since she was looking down. "Worst? There's no such thing." He paused for a moment. "What's that saying they have about fishing?"

Mac laughed a little. "The worst day fishing is better than the best day at the office."

The drummer snapped his fingers and pointed at Mac. "That's the one." He turned back to Megan. "I get to play the blues for a living." He nodded emphatically. "'Nuf said."

"But the life of a musician," the journalist replied. "It's not the easiest."

Spats cocked his head back. "Easy? No one ever said it was going to be easy." He glanced at the empty stage where his snare drum was still set up. "I take my gear from town to town, bar to bar, joint to joint, and bang my heart out pretty much every day of the year. Not every place is as nice as Pixie Point Bay, not by a very long shot."

Megan looked at him for the first time since the questions had started. "So you're in it for the love of the music?"

Now Spats guffawed. "Well it ain't the money," he declared.

"Speaking of the money," Megan said.

"Let's not," Spats said, cutting her off. Then he flashed a toothy grin at her. "Thanks for being so quick."

Maris's brows rose at the deft but very final conclusion to the interview. Megan must have heard it too.

She closed her notebook. "Thank you for your time, Mr. Thackery."

Without a glance to anyone else, she turned on her heel and went to Alfred, opening her journal again.

Mac indicated the stage. "Can I help you with the drum?"

Spats clapped the younger man on the shoulder. "Oh no, but thanks just the same. That little snare is something I could carry in my teeth."

"All right," Mac said, extending his hand. "Well, I don't want to hold you up. Just wanted to say how much we enjoyed the show."

"We really did," Maris added.

"Now that's what I call music to these ears," he said smiling as he shook Mac's hand again. "Thank you."

10

———

Outside, in the late afternoon sun, Maris and Mac crossed the still bustling Towne Plaza. Yet another group was playing in the red gazebo, Bowdie was signing autographs in a booth, and Eugene was serving BBQ buyers at the restaurant's tent. But as evening approached, Maris needed to get back to the B&B and prepare for the Wine Down.

"What was your favorite band today?" Mac asked her.

Maris pursed her lips and thought. "Well, Bowdie is obviously an amazing guitar player, but...I think the acoustic group inside, the one with Spats, has to be my favorite." She smiled. "Or maybe I just liked the songs."

Mac smiled back at her. "Sometimes they go together."

"And you?" Maris asked him, as they stepped up to the sidewalk.

"Same," he said. "That band's energy, how in sync they were, it all added up to an amazing bunch of songs."

Because regular parking was not to be had anywhere in Pixie Point Bay, Maris had arranged with Ryan Quigg for them to park in one of the spaces behind his fishing and tackle shop. As they approached Castaways, Maris saw Zarina on the sidewalk.

"Maris," she said, as they all came to a stop outside Castaways. "Good to see you."

Although her enormous glasses dwarfed her face, they only made her dark eyes seem larger. As usual, the older woman wore her brunette hair up in a bright, floral head scarf. Maris guessed her to be about the same age as Millicent, the president of the crochet club where she had met Zarina—putting her in her late seventies or early eighties.

"Zarina," Maris said, "you're looking very well." She indicated Mac. "Have you met Mac McKenna?"

Zarina extended her hand. "I only know our sheriff by his fine reputation." She smiled brightly at him as he gently took her hand.

"My pleasure," he said.

"Zarina and I sometimes crochet together," Maris said. She nodded at the club's building, which was also Millicent's house. "At By Hook or Crook."

"Crocheting," Mac said. "My mother crocheted. I still have a few of her things."

"Oh," Zarina said, her face lighting up. "Thread or yarn?"

Mac's brows drew together. "You know, I'm not sure." As he cast his eyes to the ground, thinking, Zarina looked at Maris but tilted her head toward Mac and gave Maris a knowing waggle of her eyebrows. By the time Mac looked up, she was gazing placidly at him. "It must have been thread, it was so small."

"Mmm hmm," Zarina intoned. "Like our Helen. How she can see those doilies that she does is beyond me." There was a brief pause as Zarina looked at the two of them. "Well, I best be off. My great grandchildren will be too big for their booties if I don't finish them soon." She beamed at Mac. "Wonderful to meet you at last." Then she grinned at Maris. "See you in the circle, young lady."

"See you later," Maris replied, before Zarina turned and trundled off toward the plaza.

Inside Castaways, a couple of shoppers were idly browsing the completely jam-packed store. Fishing gear of every type either hung, was shelved, or binned from floor to ceiling. In the corner there was a manikin dressed in a pair of large rubber boots with an apron that came up to the chest. Around its neck there were at least half-a-dozen wicker baskets and canvas shoulder bags, and it also wore a floppy hat.

Although she and Mac could have proceeded through and exited the back door to get to his truck, they both paused.

"Where is he?" the sheriff asked.

"Here," Ryan said, his muffled voice coming from behind the glass counter. His hands appeared at the top of the display box first, then the red hair pulled back in a pony tail, and then he hoisted himself up. "Hi."

"Ryan," Maris said, looking at the concerned look on the young man's face. "Is everything all right?"

He looked down at the floor behind the counter. "Kind of," he said. Then he looked at the glass case and craned his head to look at the floor on the other side of it. He finally turned his gaze to them. "I've misplaced a bag of sinkers."

"Oh?" Mac said, stepping forward. "Where did you last see them?"

The hair on the back of Maris's neck rose. She'd been hoping to keep the investigation into the series of thefts to herself. But it seemed that Mac had already slipped into sheriff mode. If he'd been in uniform he'd have his notepad out.

"It was right here on the counter," Ryan said pointing to the spot. "At least, I think it was."

The sheriff nodded. "With everything else being equal and without overthinking it, what would you have normally done with it?"

The store owner thought for a moment. "I'd just have fetched the bag of weights from the box back here, put it on the counter, put the box away, then put the sinkers in the right bin." He nodded to the far wall. "In that gray tray labelled one ounce disc sinkers."

But as Mac turned to see the intended destination, something on the floor caught Maris's eye. She stooped low to pick it up. It was a skinny, almost cylindrical lead weight.

"Is this one of them?" she asked.

Ryan held out his hand and Mac watched her deposit it in his palm. But the young man only frowned down at it. "No. I mean it's a sinker, but not a disc sinker." He scratched his head. "But where did it come from?"

All three of them scanned the rest of the floor, but Maris had spotted the only item to be found.

"Oh wait," Ryan said and looked up at the ceiling. "It must have fallen from there."

To Maris's surprise, the ceiling held a large collection of rods and reels suspended under its entire expanse. There were long, elegant poles with giant circular reels, regular poles like the ones used on the pier, and even some tiny ones in bright rainbow colors that must be meant for kids.

"Wow," Mac said. "That's quite the display."

Ryan pointed. "From that one." He looked at Mac and Maris. "Can you see it?" He went over to stand right under a particular one. "There are the hooks, but look at the line. It's missing this weight."

How he could have picked out the single pole that was missing something, Maris couldn't fathom. She could barely make out the clear nylon thread where he pointed. "Could it have come untied?"

The young man shrugged. "I guess it must have." He tossed the weight lightly in his hand. "It's definitely not the heaviest one I carry, but still, it's a good thing no one was standing under it."

Maris almost winced at the thought of it landing on someone's head. "That would have been an unwelcome little surprise."

"But that doesn't tell us where your bag of sinkers went," Mac said.

The three of them paused and stood gazing around the shop. With all of the merchandise displayed in every nook and corner, a bag of sinkers might be anywhere.

The two shoppers who appeared to be together brought over a boxed set of lures.

Ryan smiled and said to Mac, "I'm sure it'll turn up. I do that a lot. Set things down, and then have no idea where they are." He turned to his customers. "Did you find everything you needed?"

Ryan headed toward the cash register, and Mac said, "Thanks again for letting us park. We'll let you get back to work."

The young man waved at him and smiled. "Any time." He took the plastic box from the young woman. "This is a great set of lures. Pretty much all purpose for saltwater. I made them myself."

Maris and Mac made their way to the back and into the short hallway.

"You made them?" the young woman said behind them, surprise in her voice.

They exited through the back door to the alley, with its parking spaces and large trash bins.

Although Mac didn't mention the missing sinkers on their way to the truck, Maris couldn't help but recall the other absent items: a crystal ball, a credit card charger, a jar of honey, an album, and now some fishing weights. There was absolutely nothing that the items had in common. But now a new thought occurred to her.

What if it wasn't the items themselves, but perhaps the owners that had something in common?

11

On the morning of the second day of the festival, Maris had made sure to show up to the kitchen extra early. But in order to ensure that breakfast would be on time, she stayed well away from the stove. Instead, she was at the butcher block.

"Is the bread ready?" Cookie said over her shoulder.

Together they had confirmed what Maris had always suspected—she was a disaster in the kitchen. But over time, they'd figured out a way that she could contribute. While Cookie did all the actual baking and cooking, Maris got the fruit and vegetables cleaned, potatoes and onions chopped, and orange juice squeezed. In the dining room she made sure the coffee and hot water were ready, and also the warming trays. This morning she was also in charge of creating the cold plate of lox, tomatoes, cucumbers, and red onions, sprinkled with capers. By the time she'd arrived, Cookie had already finished the blueberry pancakes.

"Here you go," Maris said as she brought the large plate of sliced bread over. Using a small juice glass, she'd pressed a hole through the center of each slice. "You know, Eggy-in-the-Basket has to be my all-time favorite."

The chef cocked an eyebrow at her. "Uh huh." On the large commercial stove, the breakfast potatoes were well underway. "Do you have the Gruyere?"

Maris nodded and headed back to the butcher block. She'd grated at least half a pound of the hard cheese. When she returned, Cookie already had a number of bread slices in pans and had cracked an egg into the hole.

"Good," the chef said, taking the bowl of cheese from her. She liberally coated the egg and bread with it.

"My favorite," Maris said, her mouth already watering. "Those smell delicious."

Cookie laughed a little and shook her head. "Are the bagels sliced?"

"Yes, ma'am," Maris said. "I'll plate them now."

Could she be blamed for having more than one breakfast favorite? Really, when you thought about it, it was Cookie's fault.

Once the plating of the bagels and slicing of the fresh melon was complete, her last task would be taking all the warming trays to the dining room. The entire buffet wouldn't fit on the sideboard, so Maris had brought in the one from the living room prior to the weekend.

"It's nice, isn't it?" Cookie asked.

"What's nice? The Eggy-in-the-Basket?"

Cookie glanced back over her shoulder, smiling. "No. All of it. Cooking for this many guests. It's always so much fun."

Maris nearly gaped at the older woman. "Fun?" This wasn't quite the word that Maris would have applied to putting on a big buffet —especially one as varied as the B&B usually served.

"Of course," the chef declared. "It really gives us a chance to stretch our wings. Normally this kind of buffet would be wasted on just us and a few guests." Her smiled genuinely beamed. "But now we get to go all out." She turned back to the stove. "It doesn't happen often enough, as far as I'm concerned."

Maris had to grin. "Spoken like a true chef."

Not half-an-hour later, both sideboards were completely covered, the coffee was in the carafe, and the sun had risen. Its dim glow began to brighten the fog outside the dining room's window.

George was the first one down, followed by the McGraths. As the parents fetched plates for their kids, George concentrated on his options.

"It's a breakfast fit for a king," he said, turning to Maris and Cookie, who both held their plates. "You must have been up since last night."

Maris had to laugh. "Not quite. But you can thank Cookie for the buffet. She does all the cooking."

George stared at the diminutive woman.

"All of it?" He gave a low whistle. "That's pretty amazing."

Cookie shook her head. "Not when you love what you do." She inclined her head to Maris. "And you have your own sous-chef."

George motioned ahead of him. The Mc-Graths were already seated and eating. "Ladies first."

Maris managed to limit herself to a single Eggy-in-the-Basket and some slices of melon. Cookie substituted the melon with breakfast potatoes. George, however, seemed to be determined to sample everything. The big man created a breakfast plate that might have been about three inches tall. As he took his seat, he was grinning, as well as humming to himself.

"I saw you at Inklings yesterday," Maris said. "What did you think of the performance?"

George had already taken a big bite of the egg surrounded with toast. He rolled his eyes as he covered his mouth with a napkin. "Almost as good as this meal." He took a sip of coffee. "They were fabulous." He turned to Cookie. "Fabulous."

She smiled and inclined her head to him.

"I think they were my favorite," Maris told him.

But as everyone dug into their breakfasts, a silence settled on the room. Even the McGrath boys seemed completely occupied with their pancakes and maple syrup. The parents had selected the bagels, lox, and cream cheese and were almost done.

"Enjoying the sights?" Cookie asked them.

The older of the boys spoke right up, surprising Maris. "We went kayaking yesterday!" His father motioned for him to lower his voice. "It was the coolest thing ever!"

Although his mother smiled at him, she said, "Finish your pancakes, otherwise we can't get going." She turned to Cookie. "Today we're going to see the redwoods."

At her words, both boys bounced in their seats, even as they quickly resumed eating.

"We couldn't have picked a better spot," Tami said. "It's so central to so many activities."

"Exactly right," the chef agreed. "I think that's what contributed to the location of the town in the first place. All sorts of wonderful places are within an hour's drive."

"You might want to pay a visit to the Cheeseman Village Dairy," Maris put in, as she sliced her melon into chunks. "They have a wonderful little tour, you can see the cows, and the ice cream is simply to die for."

"Ice cream!" the two boys echoed.

"All right," their father said. "Upstairs and get your backpacks."

If Maris wasn't mistaken, little cartoon curlicues trailed after them as they zipped out of the dining room and into the hall. She could hear them running up the stairs.

"I'd better go make sure they get everything," their father said, as he and his wife got up. "Thanks for the delicious breakfast."

"Yes," Tami said, picking up the family's plates. "Everything was so fresh. It really was wonderful." The sound of feet pounding upstairs was followed by peals of laughter. She smiled a little. "I guess I'd better go."

"Have a nice day," Maris said.

As she left, George stood and went to the sidebar for a second helping. By the time he'd filled his plate again, Cookie had finished her tea. But rather than get up and take her plate to the kitchen as she usually did, she sat and occasionally stole a look at

George, smiling. Maris suspected that the chef enjoyed watching him eat with gusto.

The chef turned to Maris. "Are you and Mac off to the festival again?"

Maris nodded as she picked up her tea. "We are." She took a sip. "I think there'll be some new groups today."

At that George looked up from his meal. "Two new groups. I've been wanting to catch both of them for some time now."

The three of them chatted about the festival for a while, and eventually Cookie got up, taking her cup and plate. Just as she was leaving, Spats and Bowdie arrived.

"Good morning," Spats said, staring at the sideboard as he clasped and then rubbed his hands. "I was afraid we'd be too late." He went directly to the sideboard and picked up a plate.

"The smell of this breakfast upstairs actually woke me up," Bowdie said. He turned to Cookie as she passed, "Good morning. It looks as good as it smells."

Cookie gave him a smile. "Good morning. Let's just hope it's worth getting up early." She headed for the kitchen.

"Early is right," George said. "I'll bet you two didn't get in until pretty late."

"That's the music life," Spats said over his shoulder. He put some potatoes on his plate. "I haven't seen Egg-in-a-Hole for years. These look perfect."

Maris had to smile at his name for the breakfast dish. "With melted Gruyere."

Spats took a bite before he'd even sat down. "Oh," he said. "I could eat this all day."

George smiled at him, his newly full plate in front of him. "I'm gonna try."

As Bowdie sat down with them, he leaned forward to pull his chair closer. But when he did, his enormous gold necklace clinked against the side of the table.

"Don't go out on the water," Spats said, as he dug his fork into the potatoes.

Bowdie frowned a little. "Who me? Why not?"

Spats eyed the gold chain. "Because if you fall in, you're gonna sink bling first."

George laughed around a mouthful of food, and Maris had to chuckle a little.

Bowdie grinned at the drummer. "Lucky for me, I don't intend to go near the water."

Spats took a couple gulps of coffee before he regarded the young guitar player. "You know I'm just messing with you. If I could afford some bling, I'd probably break my neck with it."

As talk turned to the festival and blues music, Maris excused herself. Cookie was no longer in the kitchen, probably starting her chores already. But as Maris rinsed her plate and juice glass, she thought of the three men in the dining room and the missing items. Though she and Mac were going to the festival later in the day, she was going to make time to do some investigating.

12

When Maris came back in the house from taking out the trash, she paused at the parlor. George was looking through the blues albums. Had it not been for the fact that one was missing, she'd have thought nothing of it. A blues fan would naturally want to see them, maybe even play them. She had stopped at the doorway and was thinking about how to begin the conversation when George noticed her.

"Say," he said, standing up. "That is one serious collection you've got there. Pretty much all the classics."

The records, probably about one hundred of them, lined the bottom two shelves of the stand that held the Victrola. Most were LPs but some were also singles.

"No doubt you recognize them," Maris said, smiling.

"Oh, of course," the big man said, nodding. "Masterpieces, most of them. It must have taken your auntie decades to collect it. If you wanted an education on the blues, you could just start at one end." He pointed to the first album and then to the last. "And go straight through."

Although Maris had been looking forward to the music festival, she'd never expected to learn so much about her aunt. She'd had no idea that the crazy records she'd played from time to time were a serious collection, years in the making. If George hadn't mentioned it, she might never have known.

"I know you're retired, George, but I don't think you mentioned your work. Was it music?"

His chuckle rumbled from deep in his belly. "Oh no, not music. Textiles."

Maris arched her eyebrows. "Textiles. Interesting. Somehow I didn't see you as a fabric guy."

"Then I'm afraid you'll have to look again," he said, heading to one of the upholstered chairs. He touched the fabric on the back. "You've got a classic jacquard here. I could tell from across the room because of the intricate and variegated pattern." He lightly ran his finger over it. "Very fine work, and very much in the style of the period." Then he pointed to the curtains. "Your lace draperies have a classic English Ivy pattern. Elegant and almost sheer, but with enough material to reduce the direct sunlight into the room."

Maris stared at the pattern as though she'd never seen it before. "I had no idea that was English Ivy. But now that you say it, of course I can see it." She gazed at the chair as well. "You know, it's always been a little fear of mine that when the time comes to re-upholster the furniture, I won't be able to find the right fabric. I can't imagine it's vintage, but still..."

"When that day arrives, call me," George told her. "I'll steer you in the right direction. You're right that this isn't the original. It'd never hold up with daily use. But there are a number of shops that make Victorian inspired cloth, exactly for this purpose. There are even some that make period replicas."

Maris smiled at him. "Well, thank you, George. I might just take you up on that—though I hope it's not for a while." She paused for a moment, considering the albums. "So your love of the blues, that's more of a hobby."

He laughed that rumbling, deep laugh again. "More like love at first listen. And now that I'm retired, I can indulge myself."

"Do you play an instrument?"

He pointed to the upright piano against the far wall. "That one right there." He grinned at her. "Care to hear a little?"

"I'd be delighted," Maris said.

But as George pulled out the bench and lifted the keyboard cover, a thought occurred to her. "I don't know the last time that was tuned. And here by the ocean..."

"Not a problem," he said, taking a seat. "I'm not a stickler for right notes." His thick fingers nimbly played a scale up and down the keys. He smiled over his shoulder at her. "Not bad at all."

The next thing Maris knew, she was listening to a him play a walking bass with his left hand. After a few measures, he added the right hand, his touch light but sure. The song shuffled through one verse and then another, before he changed it up with what seemed like an improvised solo. Despite the few out of tune keys, the music was absolutely delightful, and George seemed as comfortable as though he'd been born playing the instrument—even an out of tune one.

She thought for a moment of how he'd talked about the album collection.

Would someone who'd stolen one draw attention to it? Would they even let themselves be seen looking at it?

Cookie appeared in the doorway, a rag in her gloved hand. She exchanged a smile with Maris, before turning her attention to George. In another few moments, Mojo appeared as well. He trotted directly over to the piano, sitting as close to George's feet as he could, despite the fact that the big man was working one of the pedals.

The music was upbeat, though not cheery, and always expressive, and by the time George played the last notes, he'd won his audience over.

"Bravo," Cookie said, as she clapped.

"Bravo."

"That was wonderful," Maris exclaimed, as she clapped.

Even Mojo gave George his tiny, tinny meow.

The big man laughed and reached down to give the pudgy cat a scratch behind the ears. "Thank you, Mojo." He twisted on the bench to see behind him. "Thank you, kind listeners."

"You play wonderfully," Cookie said. "It's so nice to have music in the house again."

George gazed around the room. "This is a great place for it too. Perfect acoustics."

Maris looked around, appreciating the parlor anew. "Well, I think we can thank Aunt Glenda for that. I haven't changed a thing."

Cookie nodded in agreement. "I've got to get back to the kitchen," she said. "But thanks very much for the musical interlude."

George got up from the bench. "My plea-sure." He closed the keyboard cover.

"You don't have to stop on my account," the chef said.

As the big man put the bench back in

place, he said, "It's time to head into town." When he was done, he looked at them. "But how about if I take a raincheck on that?"

Maris grinned at him. "You've got it."

13

Back upstairs to do a bit of vacuuming, Maris happened to glance out the windows facing the front of the B&B. Although she'd been under the impression that Bowdie had left around the same time as George, his car was still parked in the gravel drive. More than that, she realized as she took a closer look, the hood was open and he was looking at the engine. Though the classic sixties era car might fit well with his blues player persona, it seemed that the older vehicle also came with some maintenance downsides.

"I wonder if I should call Jude?" she muttered.

The mechanic and owner of Flour Power Sandwiches & Gas was a wizard with all things auto related. He'd even gotten Maris her current car. If Bowdie was meant to perform today—which based on the poster and schedule he was—he might need to get some help.

But as she watched the musician duck his head under the hood, Bear's truck appeared in the distance. It slowly approached, winding down the long drive from the coast highway. Though Bowdie must have heard the tires crunching on the gravel, he didn't look up. He had his hands in the engine doing something. Bear parked next to him and got out.

Maris watched as their outsized handyman came over, hands in the pockets of his bib overalls, and looked at the engine. He and Bowdie seemed to exchange a few words, and the musician pointed at something. Bear stuck his head under the hood, close to where the guitarist had pointed. Then he too reached in to do something. For several moments it seemed as though the engine compartment had swallowed the two men up to the waist, but finally Bear stood up. They chatted for a while, still staring at the motor. She'd been about to stop watching and get back to cleaning, when Bear motioned to the steering wheel and said something to Bowdie.

The musician went to the driver's side and got in, while Bear went to his truck.

"Oh," she said. "Maybe he just needs a jump."

But then Bear returned with a tool that Maris couldn't make out.

"Maybe a screwdriver?" she said lowly. "Or a wrench?"

She had no clue about engines, let alone what tools were used on them.

Bear took up a position at the car's engine where the musician had been. While he kept his eye on Bowdie, the handyman reached over to the motor with the tool. With his other hand, he gave Bowdie a signal. Even through the closed window, Maris could hear the engine fire up. Bear stood back for a few moments, just looking at the engine. Then he pocketed the tool, lifted the hood and stowed it's support, then closed it.

By that time, Bowdie had gotten out and said something to Bear, reaching out his hand. But before the big man could grab it, the musician quickly took it back, looking at it. He rubbed his two hands together, but then shook his head.

Bear went to his truck and brought back a rag, which he handed to Bowdie, who wiped his hands. The handyman did the same, and the two men shook hands.

There was a brief exchange of words, and then Bowdie climbed in the classic car and backed away. As he made his three point turn, he gave Bear a wave and headed up the drive.

The handyman waved back, went to his truck, and got his tool bag.

Among all the other things that Bear managed to do around the lighthouse and B&B, Maris would now have to add the titles mechanic and Good Samaritan.

14

A quick check of the clock on the mantle of the fireplace in the library told Maris it was time to get ready. Mac was picking her up again for the festival. If she started now, she'd have plenty of time to dither about which outfit was most flattering. But as she entered her room, she was brought up short.

Megan Kantor was there.

Even with her back to Maris, her red hair was unmistakable. Although Maris couldn't be sure, it looked as though she'd just closed the middle drawer of the dressing table. Maris went still.

Let's just see what she's looking for, she thought.

But it appeared she'd finished with the

dressing table because she turned to the door. Rather than try to jump back out of sight, Maris simply stood there.

"May I help you?" she asked.

Though she'd anticipated startling the snooping journalist, Megan simply raised her gaze and looked at her. Her narrow face didn't show the least surprise—or even an ounce of embarrassment. "Is this your room?"

Maris took a step in. "In fact it is. And this part of the house is–"

"I got lost," Megan said. She hooked a thumb over her shoulder. "I was in the lighthouse and realized there were two doors. I went through the wrong one, I guess. I found myself in some kind of laundry room, and then in here."

Unfortunately, that was only too plausible. The lightkeeper's house had been attached to the lighthouse not long after it was built. The other door, that led to the side yard and Cookie's garden, was the original.

"You can exit this way," Maris said, indicating the door behind her.

"Good," the older woman said, and brushed past. Without a word of apology or backward glance, she simply went out into the hall. Maris could hear her footsteps steadily retreating.

Now that she thought of it, Megan hadn't been at breakfast this morning.

Had she been snooping this whole time?

Maris went into the hallway and saw that the journalist had disappeared, but she paused when she looked at the nearby door to Cookie's room. They had never worried about security or privacy and, like her own bedroom door, Cookie's was open. She went to it and peeked inside. Everything seemed neat and in order. But as she backed out, she pulled the door closed. When she went back to her room, she entered, closed the door, and locked it. It couldn't hurt to be too careful.

15

On the second day of Blues on the Bay, the crowd in the Towne Plaza was even bigger. Maris and Mac stood nearer to the red gazebo today, so she could see.

"I guess they're staying in Cheeseman Village," he said, smiling.

"Oh?" Maris said, grinning. "What makes you think that?"

All five of the young musicians were wearing the distinct, yellow, cheese wedge hats that the dairy sold.

The band started their next song, a loping and lilting tune. The lead singer played mandolin, backed by a standup bass, a fiddle, banjo, and guitar—all acoustic. Unlike the thrumming music of the other blues bands, this group had more of a country vibe to them. The singer's high, reedy voice implored the blue moon of Kentucky to shine on. When the song finished to a rousing round of applause, Maris leaned in toward Mac.

"I wouldn't have thought this kind of music was called the blues," she said.

He nodded as he clapped. "More bluegrass really. But in the end, it all falls under the rubric of the blues."

Maris looked around at the appreciative audience. Clearly they thought so too.

Not a yard away from them, Bowdie stood clapping as well. She gave him a little wave when he noticed her. Then he came over to join her and Mac.

"Great group aren't they?" Bowdie said.

"Super fun to listen to," Maris said.

Mac nodded. "Amazingly talented, especially for such youngsters."

Bowdie watched them as they left the stage. "They're all from the same extended family. The singer and banjo player are brother and sister. The rhythm section are their cousins. They've all been playing together since they could hold instruments. As I recall, both sets of parents come from musical families too."

"Ah," Mac said. "A musical pedigree. Well that would explain it." He paused for a moment. "And you, Bowdie. Do you have a musical pedigree too?"

The guitarist ran his hand through his hair and chuckled. "Not at all. In fact, I guess you could say I'm a musical mongrel. Neither of my parents played an instrument. My earliest recollection of the blues is from friend's records and the TV. Hearing those songs was like hearing a door open."

"And you stepped through," Maris said.

"Oh, I jumped," Bowdie agreed. "With both feet." He paused for a moment. "And never looked back really. It's the only thing I've ever done."

"It helps to be talented," Mac said.

Bowdie laughed off the compliment. "Talent's overrated. But being in the right place, at the right time? You can't buy that." Hands in pockets, he shrugged. "It's like Johnny Mathis said. 'It's just that some people are lucky.'"

"Lucky," Mac said, smiling at the quote. "Well, I can't disagree with you or Johnny on that. Luck trumps just about everything." He checked his watch and regarded Maris. "I could use some lunch. How about you?"

"Definitely," Maris said. It was getting close to one o'clock.

Mac scanned the plaza. "I see Delia's Smokehouse has a booth. How does that sound?"

"Perfect," Maris said.

"Bowdie," the sheriff said, "can I buy you lunch?" He grinned at the younger man. "Always happy to support the arts."

"Well, now that you mention it, I think I could eat something." He gave Maris a little grin. "Then again, I think I could always eat something."

"If you want to wait in the shade," Mac said to her, "I'd be glad to go get it."

Maris smiled at him. This was definitely something she could get used to. "I'm always happy to wait in the shade."

Mac nodded. "Good. Do you know what you might like?"

Though Maris practically knew the menu

by heart, she wasn't sure what Eugene might have at the booth. "I'll have whatever you're having."

"Great," he said. "We'll be right back."

16

———

As Maris moved toward the shade cast by the gazebo, she saw someone on an intercept course—and bristled. The woman had nerve, Maris thought. She would have to grant her that.

"Maris," Megan said, approaching her, journal in hand. "I'm glad I saw you."

Maris couldn't return the sentiment. "Megan. What can I do for you?"

"I understand there have been a couple of thefts in town," the journalist said. "Is that normal for Pixie Point Bay?"

Maris did her best not to show surprise as her mind raced. Could any of the magick folk have mentioned the missing items to her? She very much doubted that. More than likely, the journalist had been eavesdropping.

"I'm afraid I don't know about any thefts," Maris said evenly.

"Someone stole some fishing weights from the tackle shop," she said, flipping through her notes. "Castaways."

"Fishing weights," Maris said, pretending to think about it. "I hadn't heard that."

"And," Megan said, turning the page, "a package of postcards from Inklings."

Now Maris didn't have to lie. "I'm afraid I didn't know about that either." She crossed her arms over her chest.

"Have you noticed any suspicious activity?"

Other than you snooping in my room? Maris thought, but said, "It's awfully crowded this weekend."

"Ah," Megan said. "So you think it's one of the visitors?" She was jotting down notes furiously.

"I didn't say that," Maris said. "Nor did I mean that."

"Is there a history of theft among the residents?"

"None of which I'm aware," Maris said.

It suddenly occurred to Maris what these scattershot questions actually were: a fishing expedition. Megan had no clue where to look or who to interview. Though irritated and wary at first, Maris relaxed.

"I've seen that the shop owners here are pretty lax about security," the journalist said. "It pretty much invites a thief to steal."

"Well, I don't know what to tell you," Maris said. "It would seem you know more about my town than I do."

The older red head slowly closed her journal and met Maris's gaze with her hawkish one. "I sincerely doubt that." Although she paused for several seconds, Maris let the silence stretch. "How long have you owned the B&B?"

"Since my aunt died," Maris said.

"In the fire," the journalist said. "Yes, I remember reading about that in my research." She seemed to be making a mental note. "And how long has your chef worked there?"

Maris frowned a little. She'd never thought of Cookie as 'her chef' or the fact that she 'worked' at the B&B. Both she and Cookie—and Glenda before her—were simply doing what they loved. Maris forced a smile. "You'd have to ask Cookie."

"I see," Megan said, casting an eye around

the busy plaza. "I suppose you know pretty much everyone here."

Again, Maris let the silence stretch, but finally said, "Not everyone."

"Really," the journalist said, smirking a little. "I'm told you manage to get around while you investigate murders. It's interesting that you and crime seem to...go together, shall we say."

More fishing, Maris thought. *Or possibly an implication*. It didn't matter. If Megan wanted to wander down the wrong line of inquiry, then Maris would let her.

"I'd have to say you're right," Maris agreed, genuinely smiling now.

"Oh?" the journalist said, blinking. "Really?"

"I do get around," she replied. "Once upon a time I opened a checking account." She pointed to the credit union. "Right over there. Another time I visited a yacht. That was at the pier. Then there was the time I took an art class."

Megan's face soured. "I see."

In fact, Maris thought, Megan did not see —not in the slightest.

Just then Minako passed them, phone in

hand, catching Megan's attention. "If you'll excuse me," she said, not waiting for Maris's reply. She trotted to catch up with her.

"With pleasure," Maris muttered under her breath.

17

Although Maris turned to see if she could catch sight of Mac and Bowdie, it was Millicent and Eunice that she saw approaching. The two older ladies ignored the musical equipment, speakers, and cables, and took their customary seat inside the gazebo. Millicent beckoned for Maris to join them.

"Maris," the president of the crochet club said. "Enjoying the festival?"

In her early eighties, she was dressed in one of her elegant silk dresses, today in peach, the long, sheer sleeves billowing as she gestured to the plaza.

"I am," Maris said, as she stepped around a microphone and then a speaker to stand at the railing near them. "Have you ladies seen any of the performances?"

Eunice, whose mouth was normally downturned, frowned a bit deeper. "Only from a distance." Unlike Millicent, she dyed her hair. This month the shoulder length curls were the color of an open flame.

"Not a fan of the blues?" Maris asked.

Eunice pushed her glasses back up her nose and peered at the surroundings. "The music is fine. It's these crowds." She shook her head. "Too many strangers in town."

"But it makes for good commerce," Maris said. "It's hard to argue with the way these strangers keep the businesses hopping."

"Yours included," Millicent replied. "I understand you're full up."

No doubt the head of the crocheting cabal knew more about the B&B's guests than Maris did. In fact, she and her cohort might know something about the thefts.

Maris nodded. "Full up is right. Two of the musicians are staying with us, along with a journalist, a young family, and a retiree." She leaned back against the railing, taking a casual pose. "Naturally there's been a good deal of talk about the festival and some about music." She paused for a moment. "In fact, it seems as though one of Glenda's blues albums seems to have been...misplaced."

Although Eunice had been glaring at the crowd around one of the autograph tables, her gaze flicked back to Maris. Millicent leaned forward, a sly look stealing across her face.

"You don't say," she said, and exchanged a look with Eunice. Millicent nodded to her.

"My phone disappeared this morning," Eunice said, her tone a bit angry. "Not that I used it much, but still."

"Your phone?" Maris asked. "Where was it?"

The thin older lady patted her enormous purse. "Where it always is—or was."

"When did you discover it was missing?" Maris asked.

Eunice glanced at Millicent before answering. "A couple of hours ago." She clutched her purse a bit closer. "Right after I was cornered by that reporter."

"Megan Kantor," Millicent confirmed. "The same woman who's staying at the B&B."

The same woman that Maris had found in her bedroom. She looked sideways to where Megan was interviewing Minako. Millicent and Eunice followed her gaze.

"Yes, that's her," Millicent said.

Eunice clucked her tongue. "Pushy and nosy. Up to no good, if you ask me."

"Very nosy," Maris had to agree.

For a few moments the three of them simply stared at her. Millicent was the first to look away.

"She goes everywhere," the head of the club noted. "She has every opportunity." Millicent nodded toward Castaways. "She had been interviewing Ryan shortly before those lead weights went missing."

So they knew about the other thefts, at least some of them. Of course they did. And they were right about the journalist likely being at each of the crime scenes.

"Huh," Maris muttered, as all three of them returned their gazes to the woman.

But what Maris couldn't fathom was what her motivation might be.

As though Eunice had heard her thoughts, she said, "Maybe she needs the money. Those shoes of hers, completely worn out."

Millicent put a hand to her chin. "Or perhaps she's a kleptomaniac." Maris regarded the older woman, who made a circling motion near her temple. "You know, maybe a bit unbalanced."

"Or both," Eunice said. She glared at the reporter for another moment or two. "Maybe I'll leave my wallet at the club the next time we're out."

"A sensible precaution," Millicent agreed.

"Ms. Leclair," Mac said, from behind Maris. She turned to see him and Bowdie, there hands full of sandwiches and cold drinks. He glanced at Eunice.

"Sheriff," Millicent said, standing. "May I introduce Eunice Harridan?" Mac inclined his head to her as she also got up.

"Ms. Harridan," Mac said, smiling. "A pleasure." He nodded toward Bowdie. "Bowdie Johnson, one of the festival's headliners."

The young man smiled at them. "Ladies."

"Lovely to meet you," Millicent said smiling, though Eunice's mouth remained down-turned. "We were just telling Maris how nice it was to see the festival be so successful." She glanced in the direction of her home. "But I think we've got to be going and find some cooler air." Eunice glared at the crowd as she descended the few steps of the gazebo. "We'll leave you to your lunch then." With a last glance at Maris, Millicent followed Eunice.

Mac handed Maris a sandwich. "Crab salad sandwiches. I hope that works for you." He gestured to the empty bench.

She smiled at him as she took her seat. "Sounds perfect."

Bowdie handed her a drink. "Sweet tea."

"Oh," she said. "That's going to be great on a day like this."

The musician smiled at her. "That's what we were thinking." He looked at Mac as they sat on either side of her. "Thanks again for lunch."

As the three of them unwrapped and dug into their meals, Maris thought back on what Millicent and Eunice had said about Megan. Something in the back of her mind was bothering her. She agreed wholeheartedly with Eunice about the woman being up to no good. Millicent was likely also right about her being at all the theft locations. It wasn't the facts that troubled her but something else...

Maris nearly choked on her crab salad sandwich when she realized what it was.

There'd been no negotiation.

When dealing with the cabal, information was currency. There was always a bit of tit for tat and secretive wrangling. But today, they'd essentially given her a freebie—and Maris knew why.

They wanted the thief caught just as much as she did.

18

As Mac backed his truck away from the B&B, Maris gave him a wave, and he gave a brief honk of the horn. She'd had a wonderful time, as usual, but both she and Mac needed to get back to work. Bowdie had another performance later in the day, so he'd decided to stay in town, and had also mentioned listening to a few of the other bands.

But as Maris closed the front door, she couldn't help but think about Megan's motivation. Millicent and Eunice had seemed to zero in on the journalist without any doubt. Although she was pushy and nosy, she simply didn't strike Maris as a thief, particularly poor, or mentally disturbed. Being gruff and not terribly likable didn't equate with stealing.

In their room, Maris found Mojo lounging. He was sprawled on the bed, but lifted his head when she came in.

"Hey there, Mojo," she said, depositing her purse next to him. She gave his soft flank a gentle pat. "Siesta time, eh?" He gave her a lazy little meow, languidly stretched, and then flopped back down. "I know what you mean."

But as she was smoothing her fingers along his fluffy fur, the room faded to a misty white—and she froze. It was a precognitive vision. Though they didn't happen often, she understood what to do now: nothing. It'd taken her some time to get used to the way her real vision disappeared without warning, but she found that if she could manage to relax, the precognition sometimes lasted longer.

A dim orange light appeared, small at first, but growing. A deepening darkness surrounded it, contrasting with the brightness at its center. But the more she looked at it, the more it looked like a flame. Yes, it was definitely a fire of some sort. It was flickering and smoke rose from it. As the circle of her vision widened, she realized there were trees. They were enormous, with deeply textured, red bark, some three stories tall.

That had to be the redwood forest east of town.

Suddenly the vision winked out, her eyesight returned, and she was looking into Mojo's amber eyes. Her hand still rested on his side but he was watching her intently. She gave him a gentle pat.

"Sorry about that, Mojo. You know how it is."

He gave her the briefest little signature meow, before getting up and jumping to the floor. As she watched him leave, she wondered about the fire. It'd definitely been in the redwood forest but it didn't seem to be burning out of control. If anything, it'd looked like a campfire.

Did she know anyone who camped?

She was heading to the armoire to change into work clothes, when she saw her purse on the bed. After what Eunice had said about her missing phone, she picked it up. At the armoire, she stashed it towards the back. It didn't hurt to be careful.

19

Finished with dusting the living room, Maris moved across the hallway to the parlor. But as she ran the duster over the coffee table and the Ouija board, she was reminded of Mojo's clue.

"Five fold," she muttered.

Neither she nor Cookie had any idea what it meant. But as she tried to puzzle it out, she looked out the bay window toward the long driveway. Bear was lifting a tool bag into the bed of his truck—and a thought occurred to her. As she exited the front door, the handyman was heading to the back of the house.

"Bear," she called out to him, stopping him in his tracks. He looked over and watched her approach.

"Maris," he said.

They stood at the corner of the house, with a view to the back and Cookie's garden, and the greenhouse. It was another warm day and the light glistening from the bay was almost blinding. She held up her hand to shield her eyes from the sun.

"I have a strange question for you," she said, still holding the duster. "Have you ever heard anyone use the words 'five fold'?"

His heavy brows drew together as he looked down at her. She watched his lips move as he mouthed the words, though he didn't make a sound. He pondered for another few moments, before he slowly shook his head.

"No," he said.

Maris sighed a little and shrugged. "Okay. It was worth a shot."

"Five is a lot," he said.

She cocked her head at him. "A lot of what?"

He shook his head and smoothed down his beard. "A lot of folds."

"Oh," she said, surprised. "I see what you mean."

"You'd have to start with a pretty big piece

of paper if you wanted to fold it five times." He thought for a second, before a light came on behind the brown eyes. "Maybe a map."

Her eyebrows flew up. "I never thought of it that way." Could something important be located on the fifth fold of a map? "A folded map," she whispered. "That's good thinking." But what map could it be? A road map? Of the town? Or maybe of the county? She glanced back at the B&B. Did they have any maps inside?

"I have the honey," he said, startling her from her train of thought.

"The what?" she asked.

"I brought more honey. Can I give it to you now?"

"Oh," she exclaimed. "Of course. How nice of you."

She followed him back to his truck, where he went to the passenger door and opened it. On the floor, in a small cardboard box that was just the right size, was the jar. He took it by its metal top and gingerly handed it to her.

"I hope you enjoy it," he said, smiling a little awkwardly.

"I'm sure we will," Maris said. "And also

our guests. Cookie and I have it in our tea." She held it up, admiring its light amber hue. "Like captured sunbeams." She regarded the big man. "Thank you."

"You're welcome," he said.

But as he turned back to close the door, Maris said, "Wait a second." Bear stopped and turned back to her. She pointed to the cardboard box. "Is that where the other honey was when it was stolen?"

He nodded. "Right there."

"Would you mind if I have a look?"

He backed up a couple of paces. "Go ahead."

She handed him the new jar of honey and the duster. "Thanks."

The small box sat on the floor mat, near the stick shift. Either Bear kept the cab of his truck immaculate, or no one rode on the passenger side—perhaps both. If there was so much as a blade of grass, a leaf, or a bit of gravel, she couldn't see it. Other than being clean, everything looked in order. Whoever had taken the honey hadn't conveniently dropped a clue. She picked up the box. Nothing else was in it, and its top flaps had been folded down inside. For a moment she thought about asking Mac to fingerprint it. But there was no guarantee that the thief had touched it, and she still didn't want to involve the sheriff if it wasn't absolutely necessary.

She was just about to set it back on the floor, when something at the cardboard rim caught her eye. When she rubbed a finger over it, it smudged. It was a tiny burn mark. She turned and showed it to Bear.

"It's been burned," she said, "but just a little."

He frowned down at it. "How was it burned?" He looked at the interior of the cab.

"I don't imagine you smoke," she said to him.

"Oh no," he said quickly. "Never."

"What was originally in the box?"

"An empty jar," he said. He held up the honey. "This one."

"Hmm," Maris said, looking at the little carbonized area. She looked up at the big man. "Would you mind if I keep it?"

He shook his head and offered her the honey, which she put in the box. Then he gave her the duster.

What it could possibly mean, Maris had no idea, but it might be evidence—and the only clue so far. "Thanks again," she told him.

20

Coming slowly down the stairs, Maris ran the duster over its elegant oak banister and balustrades. Despite its many years of use, the golden wood gleamed. Like the vintage furniture, it had been well cared for. Maris made a mental note to check with Cookie and Bear about whether there was a schedule for varnish or polish. It might be the type of project she'd like to tackle.

But as she took another slow step downward, she saw Mojo pass by the bottom of the stairs. Though it wasn't unusual to see her little black cat in the hallway, she was pretty sure she'd never seen him carrying a toy before.

Was he taking it to his secret stash?

Moving as quickly and quietly as she could, she went down the rest of the steps and peeked into the hall. He was heading toward their room. She followed him, watching him disappear through the door. Tip-toeing as fast as possible, she hurried to the bedroom and just saw his tail vanish into the utility room on the other side. Trotting now, she went to the doorway, only to find him sitting on the door to the basement. Toy still in mouth, he calmly looked at her.

She put her hands on her hips. "Seriously? The basement?"

They'd been there several times and she'd never seen anything that resembled a pile of toys.

But in answer, he dropped the stuffed toy in front of him—a googly-eyed green frog wearing a little pink bow—and gave her a loud, tinny, and insistent meow.

Maris frowned at him, then blew out a breath. "I'll get the key."

THE BIG BLACK skeleton key turned the lock's gears. The familiar grinding noise filled the quiet room, echoing a bit, until there was a final clunk. Mojo cocked his head down at the door as the key began to turn freely. As Maris grasped the handle, he picked up his stuffed frog.

"You're about to go for a ride," she warned him, and began to lift the wood door.

Not only did he not seem to get the hint, he remained on the door until it seemed he would have to slide off. But at the last possible moment he lightly leapt down, and disappeared down the stairs into the dark.

"Wait," she called after him, determined to see his stash. Quickly, she trotted down the first few steps, hit the light switch, and saw him at the bottom of the stairs. Then he darted off.

Moving fast, she headed to the bottom, keeping an eye on him. As she stepped to the floor, she turned to follow him and saw him leap up onto the antique dresser—where he came to a stop and took a seat.

"The dresser?" she said, striding over to stand in front of it.

How could he possibly open it?

As she paused to consider the little puzzle, it slowly dawned on her what she'd done.

She glanced back at the steps, which she'd practically run down. A cold shiver raced down her spine as she pictured herself simply marching into the enclosed space. Though the ceiling wasn't particularly low, looking up at it made her heart beat faster. She pursed her lips and took a deep breath. Only seconds ago, when she'd been worried about losing sight of Mojo, she'd been fine.

Was that the key to avoiding her mild claustrophobia? To have a purpose? Or simply something else to think about?

A tiny thud from the dresser startled her. With a hand over her heart, she turned to see that Mojo had dropped his toy again. He gave her his signature meow.

"Okay, okay," she said. "I'm opening the drawer."

Though she'd noticed the dresser on previous visits, she'd never taken the time to investigate it. She'd come down here to get a glimpse of Mojo's secret stash, but she also had Glenda's pendulum in mind. Though she'd found its box in her aunt's room, the pretty green stone was gone. Even now she still held out hope that it would someday reappear.

As she opened the top drawer though, it was neither the pendulum nor Mojo's toys that greeted her. Instead, it was a stash of a different kind.

"Posters," she said, taking out the short stack. "Blues on the Bay."

After what Helen had told her, it made sense. No doubt Glenda had kept them as mementos of the festival she'd helped to found. Maris rifled through them, in reverse chronological order, going back to the very first festival. With a strange sense of history repeating itself, she imagined her aunt coming down to this very spot at the end of every year's event and depositing them. She smiled a little to herself. Now she would be the one to add to the pile. She put them back in.

As she grasped the drawer handle to slide it back in, something in the front corner caught her eye, glinting. She slid the drawer out even further and had to gasp.

"The silver chain," she whispered.

She snatched it out and held it up to the long fluorescent lights overhead. There was no doubt about it. It was completely unique.

This was the silver chain from which the pendulum had hung.

About a foot and a half long, it was thick, composed of a tiny floral motif of woven flowers and minuscule leaves. The ornate ball clasp was hollow and at least a quarter inch in diameter. Though it could use a good polish, Maris would recognize it anywhere.

Eagerly, she took out the posters again, pulled the drawer as far open as it would go, and ran her fingers around the bottom of it.

Nothing.

Quickly, she opened the drawers below it. One after another she rummaged through lace tablecloths and napkins, a collection of baby clothes, some beautiful scarves and handkerchiefs, and finally packages of silk stockings. Under any other circumstance, Maris might have happily looked through all of the interesting finds. But now she had but a single goal in mind. Though she searched each of the drawers completely—twice—the pendulum simply wasn't there.

She blew out a breath as she slowly closed the bottom drawer and finally stood.

Again she held up the silver chain.

How had it gotten separated from the pendulum?

As she tried to imagine what might have happened, she suddenly realized that Mojo was no longer on the dresser.

"Hey," she said, turning to look around her. He was sitting on the stairs, watching her, with no toy in sight. She put a hand on her hip. "Wait a minute. What happened to that toy?"

In answer, he simply spun around and bounded up the stairs.

"Good grief," she muttered, hurrying over. "Wait for me."

21

As Maris was taking the silver chain to the kitchen where they kept the polish, the front door opened and Bowdie came through. For a moment she recalled the lunch they'd shared earlier in the day. But now she also remembered that even earlier, she'd watched Bear help him start his car. As she put the two images together, a thought occurred to her. She paused as he closed the door. With none of the other guests here, Maris saw her opportunity.

"Bowdie," she said, smiling. "The performances must be over."

He smiled back at her. "Yeah. I think I've seen my fill too. Or at least my feet are telling me that." He took a deep breath. "It's time to kick back for a bit."

"That sounds good," she agreed. "By the way, I wanted to ask you about what you thought of the sandwich from Delia's Smokehouse?"

His face beamed. "Oh, it was excellent! I had the Shrimp Po' Boy. Wow, what a meal. It had the cole slaw right in with the shrimp. Super tasty."

"Good to hear," she said. "I know I'm a fan of Delia's but I like to keep tabs on what others think. It helps me make recommendations when people ask."

"Well it gets a big thumbs up from me," he said. "And that was very nice of your friend to buy lunch."

"Mac is wonderful," Maris said, smiling. "You'd never suspect that he's the Medio County Sheriff."

Bowdie's eyebrows arched. "Mac? He's a sheriff?"

"*The* sheriff," Maris corrected. "For the entire region."

"Oh wow," Bowdie said. "You're right. You'd never know. He seems so laid back."

She grinned. "He is laid back. That's what Pixie Point Bay does to you." She glanced at the open door to the parlor. "But he's also a blues fan, as you know. In fact, yesterday he noticed that one of the more collectible albums in the parlor was missing."

Bowdie's smile slipped just a little. "Oh really? You don't say."

"Of course I told him that, with all the blues folks at the B&B right now, it's just been misplaced."

"Right," Bowdie said quietly. "Right."

"But he's a law enforcement officer, through and through," she said. "Next thing you know, he'll be fingerprinting that entire room."

"Fingerprinting?" Bowdie said, trying to sound nonchalant but not succeeding. "I mean, seriously?"

Maris nodded. "Oh yes. He liked that album." She watched as a tiny bit of sweat glistened on the thin man's furrowed brow. "Of course as soon as it turns up—as I'm sure it will—he'll drop the whole thing."

Bowdie rubbed his chin. "I see."

Maris pretended to fidget with the silver chain. "Well, I was headed to the kitchen for some polish. Is there anything that I can get for you before I go to vanquish some tarnish?"

Bowdie had been staring at the parlor. "Uh, no. Thanks." He headed toward the stairs. "I think I'll just lie down for a bit."

22

In the kitchen, Maris took the silver polish from under the sink, fetched a couple of rags, and went to work on the counter. Working on one small section of the silver chain at a time, she carefully applied the thick paste in tiny back and forth motions. Once the polish was wiped off, the gleam of the metal provided immediate gratification. This was how she remembered the chain, each bunch of flowers shining.

"There you are," said Megan from the doorway.

Suppressing a sigh, Maris smiled instead, and looked over her shoulder at the approaching journalist. "Megan. The festival must be over for the day."

"The music's done for today, but the work

doesn't stop." She focused her hawkish gaze on the silver chain for a moment, then looked around the kitchen, before returning her attention to Maris. "Would you mind if I ask you a few questions about the lighthouse?"

"Not at all," Maris said, dabbing a bit more polish on the next section of the chain. "Go right ahead."

Megan opened her journal. "When was it built?"

"The lighthouse itself was built in 1885," Maris told her.

"Who built it?" the journalist asked as she made a note.

"The town of Pixie Point Bay commissioned its design and paid for it."

"Hmm," Megan said, flipping back several pages in her journal. "Let's see. So the town was founded in 1771 by Wicca practitioners who'd fled the witch trials."

Maris looked at her. "I didn't know that."

Although Megan didn't look up from her notes, she nodded. "That's according to Alfred Page over at Inklings. But it's his wife who's the historian." She flipped back another page. "Right. It was a colony back then, whose location has since been lost." The journalist peered back at her. "The lost Pixie Point Bay Colony of 1771. Apparently no one seems to know where it was actually located."

"Really," Maris said, interested. "I've never heard any of this."

Megan smirked a little. "It took some digging. But a Wicca colony that magically disappears? That's a good one."

The last thing that the town would want is someone associating magic with it, so Maris decided not to comment rather than risk drawing attention to it.

The journalist turned back to the page where she was making new notes. "Okay, so it took about a hundred years for the colony to get its act together and build a lighthouse." Maris forced herself not to frown. She wouldn't have phrased it quite that way. "The bay has probably always been a natural harbor. It'd make sense in terms of money to keep the ships coming and going."

This part of the lighthouse's story was something Maris did know. "Ships that entered the harbor were charged a tonnage tax of one penny per ton, collected at the pier. It helped to pay for the upkeep and the lightkeeper."

Megan rapidly jotted all of that down. "Interesting." She looked up at Maris. "And the lightkeeper's house?"

"Built five years after the lighthouse, in 1890. But the two weren't connected until six years later."

The journalist nodded as she wrote. "Got it." She paused for a moment, and gazed around the kitchen. "And have there been a lot of modifications?"

Maris tilted her head a bit. "Not as many as you might think, and mostly for functionality. The electrical system and plumbing." She indicated the large commercial refrigerator, range, and double ovens. "The kitchen has seen the most upgrades over the years. Although the decor is Victorian, the appliances are most definitely modern."

The journalist noted that down. "So, it's not a historic landmark."

"Correct," Maris confirmed.

"And the lighthouse?" Megan asked.

Maris shook her head. "It's not a landmark either. The previous lightkeepers never sought that designation. As far as modifications, there've definitely been some for the sake of safety and continuous operation. For example, the light is provided by LEDs now, instead of an oil lamp."

"An oil lamp," Megan said, smiling a little, as she made a note.

"We still have it, actually. My Aunt Glenda kept it."

That made Megan pause. Then she flipped back through the journal. "That reminds me. Something about that fire. Something I heard." She stopped and ran her finger down the page, reading. "Uh huh. The previous lightkeeper was killed."

Maris set the chain aside and recounted how Glenda had died. She'd come back to Pixie Point Bay for the funeral, and decided to stay.

"And what did you do before that?"

"I worked in the hospitality industry," she replied. The longer she was here, the less she thought about that previous career. At this point, she couldn't remember the last time it came to mind. "I spent a couple of decades trotting the globe for Luguan Imperial Resorts."

Megan nodded as she scribbled a few notes. "Impressive. I stayed in one once." She looked up at Maris. "We might even have crossed paths. Were you ever at the one in Manhattan?"

Maris smiled at her. "No." Which meant it must have been run pretty well. "They're headquartered in Miami."

Megan nodded. "So you own the lighthouse and B&B now," she said. "You inherited it."

Maris nodded. "That's right."

"Interesting," the journalist said as she made a note. "Pretty nice inheritance." There was no disputing that, but Maris decided not to go into the details. The journalist smirked. "It'll be a matter of public record—the value of the property and the circumstances around your aunt's death."

Maris pointedly picked up the chain again. "Of course it will." She used the rag to dab more polish and applied it to the next section. "No doubt you've worn a rut to wherever those sorts of records are kept."

"Let's just say the sites are bookmarked on my computer," the journalist replied. "I might also have a few numbers on speed dial."

Megan closed her journal and snapped the rubber enclosure around it, but didn't turn to go. When Maris gazed up at her, she'd stashed the notebook under her arm and was looking out the window. Though not as expansive a view as the bay windows gave, it nevertheless looked north along the rugged and undulating coast. Because its location on the rocky promontory gave the lighthouse an ideal placement, the views from any of the B&B's windows were pretty stupendous.

At the moment, the sinking sun was bathing the buff cliffs in a soft rosy glow. The water below them had turned Prussian blue, with just a thin line of white surf against the shore.

"A truly magical location," the journalist muttered. "I'm hard pressed to think of another quite like it."

"Thank you," Maris said simply.

As though startled from her thoughts, Megan peered at her. "Any idea where your chef is?"

Maris shook her head. At this time of day Cookie might be in her garden, or perhaps the greenhouse. But the last thing that Maris would inflict on her was a Q&A session with the reporter.

"I'm afraid not," she said. "Cookie handles

the breakfast buffet, and I put on the evening wine and cheese, which will be in about an hour, by the way."

Megan took another look around the kitchen, then turned to go. "Thanks for your time."

"My pleasure," Maris lied.

23

On the following and final day of the three day festival, Maris and Mac weren't attending. Though he would have liked to and she certainly wouldn't have minded, civic duty and hospitality would wait for no man or woman. With another breakfast buffet done and the dishwasher running, it was time to collect the trash.

But as Maris passed the parlor, she paused. Everyone but her and Cookie were gone, and ample time had passed since her quick conversation with Bowdie. She decided to do a quick check. As she crouched down in front of the album collection, she quickly flipped through the records and had to smile. The missing album had returned.

As she reached for it, a tiny, tinny meow drew her attention to the door. Mojo stood there, his big orange eyes fixed on her.

"Hey there, Mojo," she said, standing.

But as she approached him, he trotted off. Out in the hallway, she saw that he had paused and was watching her over his shoulder. He gave another meow, before disappearing into the living room.

She knew a summons when she heard one.

MARIS FOLLOWED Mojo to the living room but stopped in the doorway.

"What in the world?" she muttered.

Crouched low with his rump in the air, he was glaring at a lump in the rug.

She'd vacuumed this room just yesterday, and there'd hardly been a wrinkle in the Persian rug, let alone a bump.

"What's going on?" Cookie said, coming up behind her.

Without a word, Maris stood aside and simply pointed to the scene in front of them.

Cookie put a hand to her chest. "Goodness. What is that?"

"I have no idea," Maris said under her breath.

Rear end in the air, Mojo waggled his body back and forth, dug his claws into the thick pile of the rug, and pointed his whiskers ahead. Slowly and silently, he stalked forward, inch by careful inch.

Without warning, he pounced.

Cookie started and grabbed Maris's arm while they both stared at the little black cat. He'd jumped into the air almost vertically and come down directly on the lump. As they silently watched, he seemed to be trampling it. Then he did something that Maris had never heard him do—he growled. It was a low guttural sound, even more alarming than his actions. It sent a quaking shudder into the pit of her stomach.

"What does he have under there?" Cookie whispered, her grip on Maris's arm tightening.

Maris shook her head. "Whatever it is, it wasn't there yesterday."

"Or this morning," Cookie agreed. "You'd better have a look."

Maris stared at her. "*Me?*"

Cookie nodded at the still growling Mojo. "He's your cat."

As Maris looked back to him, he jumped up in place and came back down on the lump. Now he seemed to be prancing in place.

"Good grief," Maris muttered. She looked down at the edge of the rug. But it was a good dozen feet to the lump. As she crouched down to take hold of the edge, Cookie backed up. Maris looked over her shoulder at her.

"What if something comes scurrying out?" the chef asked.

Maris grimaced. She hadn't thought of that.

Good grief.

She wouldn't mind backing up now too. But as Mojo continued to growl and stomp, she knew she had to look.

"Hurry," Cookie urged her.

"Okay, okay," she muttered.

But if it was some kind of rodent, she was going to scream.

Slowly, she lifted the edge of the ornate rug. It wasn't as heavy as she'd expected, but without the light from the windows on the other side of the room, it was completely black underneath. A tiny lump of fear settled in her stomach and anxiety tightened her chest. A claustrophobic attack had been the last thing Maris had expected. But as she continued to lift the rug, creating more of a dark cavern below it, she understood why.

But then she had an idea. Instead of lifting it, she lowered it back to the floor.

"What are you doing?" Cookie asked.

"I am not crawling under there," Maris said. She grasped the edge of the carpet and began to roll it. "Cookie," she said, "can you scoot that ottoman out of the way?"

The chef darted forward, shoved it aside with her foot, and sprang back into the hallway. Though Maris knew that Cookie was spry and particularly fit for her age, she was still impressed. "Nice scooting."

Bent over almost double, Maris pushed the growing roll toward the lump. The more rug she gathered in the uneven roll, the larger it became and the faster it went. In her anxiety to just be done with this, she was moving too fast. She was creating a tidal wave of fabric.

"Mojo," she shouted. "Look out!"

The fluffy black cat looked up at her and saw the approaching wall of rolling rug. His orange eyes got huge.

"Mojo, move!" Cookie yelled.

Maris sank to her knees and grabbed the roll, trying to stop it, but only managed to slow it. Mojo leapt straight up into the air again, landed on the roll as it finally came to a stop, and then leapt down to the bare floor.

"Oh my god," Cookie whispered. "*What is that?*"

Without looking, Maris scrambled to her feet and jumped backward. She stared down at what the rug had revealed and could hardly believe it. It was a giant red spider the size of her hand.

Mojo leapt at it.

"No!" she exclaimed, reaching out a hand to stop him, but it was too late.

He snatched it up in his jaws, swung his head back and forth, and tossed it at the door —where Cookie shrieked. Maris charged forward, scooped up her cat, and then brought her foot down hard on the red insect. But to her shock, she didn't squish it. All she felt was a sort of cushy softness that gave way. As Mojo cocked his head at her foot, she stared down at it too. The spider's red limbs, striped with black, were splayed out in all directions around her shoe.

"Did you get it?" Cookie said from the far side of the hall, her back against the wall. "Is it dead?"

But the more Maris stared down at the floor, the more she understood what it was. The limbs were fuzzy, but not in a spider fur kind of way. If she had to guess, she'd say it was terry cloth. Slowly she lifted her foot, and felt the 'spider' spring back into shape. She stepped back and smirked at it.

"Yeah, it's dead," she said, and smiled at the chef. "It's a toy."

Cookie exhaled. "Oh, thank goodness. A toy."

Mojo squirmed to be put down and Maris lowered him to the floor. As soon as she let go of him, he grabbed the spider in his jaws and scampered from the room. She could hear him galloping down the hallway.

Cookie shook her finger at him. "Next time, young man, I'm going to send you in after it." Then she lowered her voice. "As soon as I'm done having a heart attack."

Maris had to chuckle. Mojo and his toys.

Next time she'd probably find one under her pillow. But at the thought of finding a spider toy there, she shuddered and had to shake it off.

She turned to unroll the rug, but she saw something else on the floor. "What's this?" she said lowly.

"Oh no," Cookie said, freezing in place. "Not more."

"It's okay," Maris said, bending down to pick it up. "It's just a card." She turned it over. "A tarot card."

"What in the world is it doing under the rug?" the diminutive chef said, finally coming into the room.

Maris shrugged. "Same thing as the toy I suppose."

Cookie tsked, but peered down at the card. "The five of pentacles."

A man on crutches and a woman clutching a shawl were trudging through the snow. Behind them was a stone wall with a beautiful stained glass window. The design featured five yellow circles, a star in each.

Maris gave her temple a little tap and brought up an image of the tarot guidebook that came with the deck. "The two people are destitute, living in poverty. The woman is in bare feet in the snow, and the man has been injured." She examined the card again. The couple really did look pitiful. "Behind them is a church, lit up from within and exuding warmth. Found in the upright position it means recovery from financial loss, or recovery from spiritual poverty." She handed the card to Cookie.

The chef examined it, turning it over once. "Financial loss." She looked up at Maris. "Could that mean the thefts?"

Maris tilted her head and pursed her lips. "It could be." She thought for a second. "Or maybe the church has something to do with it. Or the stained glass?"

Cookie sighed. "Right."

Maris turned back to the rug and, using her foot, unrolled it all the way back to the door. "Next time Mojo has a tarot clue for us, I hope it won't be so much work." She checked her watch. "Or time consuming. I thought today would be my catch-up day."

"You're not going to the festival?" Cookie asked as they left the room.

Maris shook her head. "Mac and I both had too much to do."

Cookie paused, card still in hand. "I know we're full up, but there's always a way to make a little time for ourselves."

Maris regarded her. "Oh really. I haven't seen you in the garden recently."

Cookie shook the card at her. "That's exactly right. You haven't seen me." She smiled. "But I always make time for it. Even just a little bit of weeding, watering, or fertilizing. I never skip it."

Maris stared at her. "Really?"

"Really," the chef confirmed. "It doesn't have to take long." She shook the card at her before turning toward the parlor. "Before you do another thing in this house, take some time for yourself." Although she'd disappeared inside, Maris could still hear her. "I always do." There was a pause. "Now where is that box?"

24

Rather than bring her watercolors out to enjoy the fine weather and sunshine, Maris decided to simply take a walk. The entire property was larger than it first appeared, because a low wooden railing fenced off most of it. For the safety of visitors and guests, particularly the children, most of the rocky promontory on which the lighthouse sat was off limits. Though scaling the rocks down to the narrow bit of sand could certainly be done, you had to be fit as well as wear the right kind of shoes. Maris contented herself with a stroll along the small white fence, as she looked down on the jagged shore.

Like the larger tide pools north of the bay,

on the scenic drive to Cheeseman Village, smaller versions dotted the natural ledges of dark rock below. Even from this distance, Maris could make out a few dots of color among the sand and seaweed, mostly deep oranges and bright blues. As a girl she'd climbed all over the area, watching the little creatures in the pools for hours. She'd then searched the field guides that Glenda kept in the library, which were still there.

"Take them with you," her aunt had urged. "That's what they're for."

Eventually she'd been able to identify some of the starfish, at least one type of crab, and the sea urchins too.

But as she walked along the fence, hands clasped behind her back, it wasn't the little ecosystem's creatures that occupied her mind —it was the thefts. She went over them again in her mind. Now that the album had been restored to its rightful place, it was down to Howard's crystal ball, Eugene's credit card machine, Ryan's weights, Eunice's phone, postcards from Inklings, and Bear's honey. Though she hadn't had the time to systemati-cally question the business owners who weren't magick folk, the pattern thus far pointed to magic practitioners losing items—sometimes items involved with magic.

"Magic," she muttered.

That had to be the connection. The items themselves were so random, or at least they appeared to be.

Was there any way to use them together? One was a machine. One was food. One was a solid rock.

"No," Maris said, shaking her head. It'd be impossible to use them together.

Or perhaps the five of pentacles tied them together. She counted up the items. There were six. So that aspect didn't jive.

As she turned back to the B&B, she was surprised by how far she'd come. She'd been completely lost in thought. But as she headed back, she had to smile. She felt less harried, less in a hurry, and much more relaxed. She shielded her eyes with her hand out to the sun. It was another gorgeous day on the bay. The only better view would be from the lighthouse.

She gazed up at it, the faceted optics house gleaming in the sunlight.

"Claribel," she said, and quickened her pace.

Though she might not have time to ask some questions in town today, there was one course of investigation of which she had yet to avail herself.

25

As Maris approached the door to the lighthouse, a warm sea breeze swirled all around her. She held her hair back from her face with one hand, and gripped the edge of the door that was opening with the other. As she moved inside, she let it go and it gently closed behind her.

"Good morning, Old Girl," she said.

Although the interior of the conical tower was lit by windows as well as the light that poured down from the top, Maris realized for the first time that it was cool inside. Despite the blazing sun outside, the temperature here was more like that of early evening. As she wound her way up the wrought iron, spiral staircase, with its ornamental black balustrades and textured steps, she thought about the temperature and looked out through the first window. Though she was often taken with the views that it afforded, today she noticed the wall in which it was set.

"Two feet thick?" she guessed. That had to help keep the temperature pretty even.

But on the second level—though it was hard to tell—the wall appeared to be slightly less thick. Finally, on the third level, the wall surrounding that window was almost a normal thickness. As the cone of the lighthouse tapered inward, the wall thinned, becoming more graceful as the building rose.

Maris had to smile at the small realization. After all this time, the Old Girl was still a surprise. As she climbed the last couple of steps, breathing a little hard but no longer having to pant, she ascended onto the metal landing and gazed around at all the glass—three hundred and sixty degrees of it. As she'd done on the way up, she took in the structure itself rather than just the views.

An elegant and finely wrought metal frame held the crystal clear windows, also known as storm panes. It made sense to her that the view ought to be as unobstructed as possible, allowing the lightkeeper to spot trouble, and those at sea to spot the beam. But she'd never really appreciated the beauty of the floor to ceiling glass itself. Bear kept the panes amazingly clean, doing the maintenance that Aunt Glenda had once done. But now Maris wondered if she wouldn't enjoy taking on some of the upkeep herself—as long as heavy lifting wasn't involved.

"Or greasy bearings," she said.

Then again, maybe it wasn't as icky as it sounded.

She crossed her arms, pondering it, as she paused to take in the view. Although the optics room was warmer than the tower below, it seemed to her that the panoramic view itself was bright and hot. So many blazing white sparkles reflected from the surface of the bay, it looked more like a mirror than water. The sky's pale blue had taken on a powdery lightness, particularly over the distant horizon. Even the craggy rocks below glistened with ocean spray, and the green of the undulating coastline was dotted with wildflowers in brilliant hues of yellow.

Maris found herself smiling in every direction. It was simply gorgeous.

Finally she turned to a sight that was

equally entrancing but in a different way—the fresnel lens. Although most people probably thought of it as the all-seeing-eye of the lighthouse, she thought of it as its heart. Complicated, multi-faceted, and filled with light, Maris considered it the core of the magical being.

"Hey there, Claribel," she said to the giant steel and glass structure.

As she gazed into its myriad of shining pieces, most etched with fine concentric circles, she let her eyes unfocus. A rainbow of tiny sparkles danced inside the glass, refracting the brilliant sunlight. They floated to and fro, some of them swirling like the sea breeze outside. But eventually, as Maris watched, they began to coalesce. They formed a scene of something she recognized.

"The festival," she murmured.

Two groups were performing in the plaza, one on the far stage and one in the gazebo. But as her view zoomed in, she was drawn to the other end of the town center. There on the sidewalk, she clearly saw Millicent. The president of the crochet club seemed to be listening to the music, though she stood at a distance, in front of her home and the club's headquarters. People milled around her and, as usual, her eagle eye seemed to notice everything.

But then the vision winked out.

Maris had to blink. For a moment, she simply stared at the fresnel lens thinking about what she'd seen. It made sense that someone who lived on the plaza might step outside to enjoy the music, and yet something about that bothered her. She recalled the many times she'd visited Millicent in her home, sitting in the crochet circle. The club president often sat in front of the fireplace, but there was no bad seat in the circle because the large front room was bathed in light.

But at its back, Maris had noticed a white baby grand piano. Though it simply looked like another piece of furniture, there was sometimes music on its stand. As her brows drew together, she tapped her temple. She could just make out the large letters of the piece's title: Piano Sonata No. 1. It had to be a classical piece.

"Hmm," Maris muttered.

So Millicent played classical piano. Could she also be a fan of blues music? No doubt music lovers simply loved music, but the two genres seemed pretty far apart. Or perhaps her interest in the festival stemmed from being on the committee. Although Maris considered it for a second, there was really only one way to find out.

Maris smiled at the glittering glass in front of her, and patted the base of the lens.

"Thank you, Old Girl."

26

As Maris exited the base of the lighthouse to the side yard, she immediately spotted Bear and Megan. She had her journal out, pen in hand, and seemed to be taking notes at a furious rate.

"Uh oh," Maris muttered, and casually strolled over.

Although Bear stood at the entrance to the greenhouse with a caulking gun in his hand, he seemed frozen in place, his head turned to the reporter.

"You say it was in your truck when you pulled in for gas?" Megan was saying.

The journalist had obviously not let go of the thefts. The woman had dogged determination.

"Megan," Maris said. "I'm surprised you're not at the festival, especially since it's the last day." In fact, she wasn't surprised in the least, but thought she'd try a hint.

The woman smirked at her. "It turns out there's more to Pixie Point Bay than blues music." She nodded at Bear. "Mr. Orsino here has been telling me about his missing jar of honey."

"Whoever has it," he said, "can keep it."

"Yes, yes," Megan said impatiently. "So you said. If someone hungry took it, they can have it. The bees always make more." She fixed him with one of her hawkish looks. "But tell me, did you report it to the sheriff?"

Maris clenched her jaw, but kept silent.

"No," Bear said simply, still holding the caulking gun as though he was ready to work on the greenhouse door.

"And why not?" the journalist asked.

Bear simply shrugged.

"No reason?" she asked.

Bear shook his head.

Although Megan tried to wait him out, Bear apparently had no more to add. Although the journalist frowned, Maris had to suppress a small smile. Megan had no idea who she was dealing with. If she was hoping to get him to say more than he wanted or coax something out of him, she might need to stand here all day. Even then, Maris had her doubts. As the journalist made a note, Maris exchanged a look with Bear, who gave her just the hint of a grin. When Megan looked back up at him, it instantly vanished. A suspicious look replaced her penetrating one, as she glanced between them.

"No matter," Megan said, closing the journal with finality. "I think I've figured out who the thief is."

Maris cocked her head back. "Oh?" A little knot of dread tightened in her chest.

The reported glanced back at the B&B and lowered her voice. "George, your retired guest."

Maris scowled at the woman. Bear however turned back to the greenhouse and pulled the long trigger on the caulk gun, applying a bead of clear caulk near the top of the door. Megan ignored him.

"George?" Maris said. "Why in the world would you think it was George?"

"He's been everywhere that there's been a

theft," the reporter declared. "Every single place."

"You realize, of course," Maris said, "that's entirely circumstantial. Do you have any evidence?" Although the keen glare had returned, Maris simply stared back at her.

"Of all the people that I've interviewed," Megan said, "and that's quite a lot, he is the only person who can be placed at all of the theft locations."

A little relieved, Maris smiled at the woman. "So that would be a 'no.' You don't have any evidence." She crossed her arms. "That might hold up for some story you'd write, but not in a court of law. You couldn't even get a search warrant based on what you know." Maris paused for a moment. "Or what you think you know."

Megan gave her an icy smile. "Well then lucky for me, I'm a writer and not a cop." She glanced at Bear's back and then at Maris. "I think I'll head to the festival now. I expect that's where I'll find George."

The woman turned on her heel and left, barely avoiding stepping on some of the plants in the garden. When she'd gone into the house and slammed the porch door behind her, Maris turned to Bear who was looking at the closed door.

"Not the most pleasant guest we've had," she said.

"No," was all he said.

But as he turned back to the greenhouse, Maris interrupted him. "Bear, I was wondering something." He stopped again and turned to her. "I was thinking that I might like to do some of the maintenance duties for the lighthouse. I remember Glenda cleaning the storm panes, for example. Is that something that I could tackle?"

He looked up at the optics house, then back to her. "You could do that, but you need a ladder to reach up high. It would be safer with two people."

"Oh," she said. She gazed up at the lighthouse's windows. "I see." Then she glanced at Bear. "I suppose you're tall enough that you don't need a ladder?"

He smiled at her. "Yes." Then he paused, and stroked his beard. "But inside the optics house, you could use a ladder."

She grinned. "So I could clean the inside of the storm panes, while you clean the outside."

He shook his head a little. "I was thinking you could clean the fresnel lens."

Maris's heart leaped into her throat, and she nearly hopped in place. "Could I? That'd be wonderful!"

His smiled broadened. "I would be happy to show you."

She beamed back at him. "It's a deal. Next time it needs to be cleaned. Agreed?"

"Agreed," he said, and turned back to the greenhouse.

Maris went to the back porch and entered just in time to see Megan heading out the front door. Her high at the thought of cleaning Claribel's lens dimmed a little. Then she thought of George. She could hardly imagine that the affable and knowledgeable retiree would be a thief.

What could he possibly want with a jar of honey or some fishing weights?

Though she didn't want to see one of her guests hound another, she was also pretty sure that the journalist was on the wrong track. It would come to nothing except a waste of time, which would give her a chance to actually find the real thief—after she finished her chores.

27

With the B&B ship-shape, clean, and toys removed from under rugs, Maris went to her bedroom. All day she'd thought about what Megan had said and her suspicions of George. She'd obviously done a lot of investigative work to be able to tie him to all the locations, but it had been Millicent who'd pointed out how suspicious the journalist behaved. As Maris entered her bedroom, she recalled finding Megan snooping in it. If she hadn't seen her leaving, Maris fully expected to find her snooping again. But the only other person in the room was Mojo.

He was curled up on the seat of the bay window, in a little patch of late afternoon sunlight. She went over to him and ran her hand down the warm fur along his spine.

"It's too hot over here," she said to him. In response, his sleepy eyes rolled to look at her, before closing again. "Bake away then, but don't say I didn't tell you."

As her thoughts returned to the reporter again, she decided to do a little investigating from the comfort of her desk. She took out her little used laptop, booted it up, and did a search for Megan Kantor.

Her name was everywhere.

It was probably to be expected, since she was a writer. Most of the web pages were articles that she had written. Often her name was linked with the Pulitzer Prize—again no surprise. But as Maris scrolled through the search results, one page after another, a strange pattern appeared. Some of the articles weren't by Megan, but rather about her. They pointed out how her gritty stories tended to feature ordinary people in extraordinary circumstances. It was a style that had gotten her the prestigious writing award. But the prize was now some decades in the past.

"Muckraker," Maris read.

Lately Megan was characterized as someone who sought out scandal in order to make it public. It was a feel-bad style of reporting and writing that was most definitely no longer in vogue. Once lauded for asking the tough questions, now her journalism was sometimes labelled inflammatory.

One critic even wrote, "Rigorous takes a back seat to scurrilous."

Maris sat back. "Hmm." The thefts weren't exactly a scandal, but could she make them seem that way? It was possible, if she tried hard enough. From what Maris had seen, trying hard was one of Megan's strong suits.

In the many times that she had been with the journalist as she'd made notes, Maris had never seen what she was actually writing. She gave her temple a tap and called up the time she'd been interviewing Bear.

Although the notebook was upside-down, Maris was slowly able to read the text—and she had to frown.

"Bear Orsino," she read. "Six foot, five inches. Heavy. Beard and short hair, light brown. Blue overalls, white t-shirt. Handyman. Too dull for a thief. Possible victim. Honey."

Possible victim? Of course he was a victim. The honey had been taken from his truck. Plus Bear was anything but dull. He might be a man of few words—very few words—but he was neither dim nor dull.

Maris tapped her temple again and called up her time with Megan in the kitchen, when the journalist had asked her about the lighthouse and B&B.

"Death by fire," the first note at the top of the page said, and Maris stopped reading.

Instead she seethed.

She had specifically told the woman exactly how Glenda had died. They were going to need to have a talk.

Just then Mojo jumped onto her lap, startling her for a second.

"Uh, come on up," she said, petting his sizzling hot back. "What did I tell you?" He gave her a plaintive little meow. "Well maybe next time you'll listen." But as she gazed at his spot near the window, she realized how low the sun had sunk. She picked him up and put him on the floor before she stood. "Time to start the Wine Down."

28

As Maris headed to the kitchen to start another fondue but with different dippers tonight, she ran across George. He was coming down the stairs with an album in his hand. But as Maris stared she realized it wasn't just any album, it was *the* album: the one that had been missing and then reappeared. Before she could ask him about it, he lumbered to the bottom of the steps and showed it to her.

"Look what I found," he said, staring at it himself. He handed it to her.

"Found?" she said. "Where?"

"Well," he said, rubbing the top of his head and glancing back up the stairs, "you won't believe it, because I sure don't. But it was in my suitcase."

Maris scowled at him. "Your suitcase?"

The big man nodded. "I'm afraid so." She stared at him, incredulous, but then realization began to dawn. If he hadn't put it there, she could guess who had. "I don't know how it could have got there."

"Well," Maris said, seething again. "It seems to have a mind of its own. It's gone missing a couple of times this weekend."

"Missing?" George asked, seeming a bit alarmed. He pointed to it. "Then maybe you'd better put it in a safe place. It's a keeper for sure."

Maris nodded. "That's what I've been told."

George regarded her. "Well, did they tell you its probably worth seven or eight thousand dollars?"

Her mouth dropped open briefly, before she recovered. She gaped at the album in her hand. "This?"

"Mmm hmm," George intoned. "That."

She turned the album over in her hands, before staring at the front again. It was done in sepia tones, but it wasn't a photo. It was a cartoon. The band was drawn playing together on a round stage, but the instruments and players were all a little out of proportion and angular.

"I had no idea," she said, finally looking up at him. "But you do?"

He chuckled a little. "Let's just say I keep tabs on the market value of a few select records."

Her brows knit together. "As an investment maybe?"

Now he laughed. "Nah. It's my ego." He held out his hand for the album, and she gave it back to him. He turned it over. "Here," he said, pointing at the credits on one of the songs.

Maris peered down at it. "Piano, Big George Brunell." Her eyes widened. "You?"

He laughed again and handed the album back to her. "Is it really that hard to believe?"

As she read the credits for the other songs, it turned out he'd been the only piano player on the entire album, playing on most of the songs. She flipped it over to study the front, and pointed to the rotund shape playing the wonky piano.

"Is this you?" she asked.

He nodded, grinning. "It's hard to recognize me because it's not my best side."

"Wow," she said, smiling at him. Then she recalled him playing on the out-of-tune upright. "And in answer to your question, no, it's not hard to believe at all." She gazed at the parlor. "But your knowledge of fabrics…"

He shook his head. "I know, I know. But I was a much younger man when this album was made. Full of vim and vigor, full of hope."

Maris looked at the vintage record it with a new appreciation, and not because of its value. "Full of talent, I'd say."

He inclined his head to her. "I thank you."

"So you were playing professionally in the early sixties?" she asked, heading to the parlor.

"Uh huh," he said, following her. "Then in the seventies I left the music biz to work in textiles. I just couldn't make a go of it." He shrugged his wide shoulders. "The endless touring. The beer stained keyboards. The chincy pay." He shook his head and smirked. "I cut my losses while I was behind." As Maris put the album back in its place, he gazed at the piano. "I still enjoy playing, and

I'm a big music fan, but trying to make a living at it was just eating me alive." He smiled at her and patted his protruding stomach. "It's hard to stay big if you can't afford to eat."

She grinned back at him. "Speaking of which, I was just about to start preparing for the wine and cheese."

He gallantly gestured to the door. "That's the last thing I'd want to delay."

AS GEORGE TOOK a seat in the living room, Maris was again on her way to the kitchen when the front door opened and Megan appeared. Heat flared in Maris's face but she smoothly changed direction and intercepted the journalist.

"Megan," she said pleasantly, "I'm glad you're back. Could I speak to you?"

The woman's sharp features showed surprise. "Of course."

"This way," Maris said, leading her to the back, out through the vestibule, and onto the back porch.

"Did you remember something about the

history of the lighthouse?" she asked, her journal in hand as always.

Maris paused at the railing and turned to her. "No. I remembered to look up your work on the internet."

That brought her up short, and her eyes became wary. "Oh yes?"

Maris crossed her arms and nodded. "Yes. Very impressive."

Megan brightened. "Oh, yes."

"So I just want to let you know that..." Megan opened her journal. "...that the album that was placed in George's luggage has now been returned to the parlor."

Though the journalist had clicked the ballpoint pen, she wasn't writing. "The album..."

"Furthermore," Maris continued, "Bear may be a man of few words, but he is neither dull nor a potential thief for your story."

Megan gaped at her. When she realized her mouth had dropped open, she closed it and the journal, and clutched the small book to her chest. "How did you read what–"

Maris held up a hand. "I haven't touched your notebook," she said truthfully but pointedly looking at it. "But there's a certain pattern to your work and a certain tone that it takes."

"Speak plainly," the journalist said, seeming suddenly impatient.

"Fine," Maris said. "I'm telling you that you're not going to find success or win any prizes by writing a negative story about Pixie Point Bay and its people. Period. And I'm even going to tell you why that's so." She paused to let her words sink in. "Because it's just not true. No amount of fiction, planted evidence, or fact spinning can make it true either. It will simply not be believable."

Megan dropped her hands to her sides. "I see. Are we done here?"

"No, we're not. I have one piece of plain-speaking advice for you. Then we're done."

Though the journalist frowned and clenched her jaw, she said, "Say it."

Maris softened her tone and did her best to muster a smile as well. "You're a talented writer. Of that there's no doubt. But consider what might happen if you saw things for what they really were, and wrote that truth. There's power in that kind of candor. Real power."

"Thanks," Megan said, biting off the

word. She turned on her heel, and strode back into the house.

Maris sighed. "Well, I tried."

29

Although the McGrath family had checked out earlier in the day, the boys already talking about their next destination, the musicians were all at the Wine Down. Soft evening light filtered in through the dining room's bay window, while lively conversation took place. The last day of the festival had apparently been as big a hit as the others.

As Maris passed Bowdie his glass of wine, she said, "How was attendance today? Was it a good-sized audience?"

He beamed at her as he took the drink. "The best yet. Today was the biggest festival attendance ever. It broke a record."

Maris grinned back at him. "That's wonderful news."

On his way to the sideboard, Spats clapped the guitarist on the shoulder. "This young man was on fire today."

"Really?" Maris said, pouring another two glasses at the table, one of red and one of white.

Just then Megan appeared in the doorway, and Maris offered her a choice by holding up both glasses.

The journalist managed a little smile and took the white. "Thank you."

"My pleasure," Maris said, inclining her head. She nodded at the guitarist. "Bowdie was just telling us that the festival set a new attendance record today."

Megan arched her brows as she sipped her wine. "Oh really?" she said.

Maris noticed that she hadn't brought her journal.

"Smashed it," Bowdie replied. "And what a great crowd."

George was just returning with a plate full of cheese-dipped vegetables and lightly toasted sourdough croutons. "Boy, that crowd was so into it today," he said. "Sort of like a last hurrah."

"I don't know what it was," Bowdie said,

setting down his glass and picking up his own plate, already half-eaten. "I don't care what it was. It was amazing." He turned to Megan. "Were you there?"

She nodded. "I was. And you're right. There was definitely a different kind of energy today."

Spats returned at that point, plate in hand. "It just sort of lifts you up when an audience responds like that. The more they got into it, the more we got into it." He popped a cherry tomato into his mouth. "Mmm, sweet."

"White or red?" Maris asked him. "I'm pouring a dry Chardonnay and a crisp Sangiovese tonight."

He glanced around at what everyone else was having. "The red please."

The conversation turned to the various performances, their favorite songs, and the new players. Maris refreshed both the fondue and the dippers, and opened more wine. It seemed the festival had come off without a hitch, and everyone was in a celebrating mood—which suited her just fine. It was great to see the festive weekend come to a pleasant conclusion.

The older drummer regarded Megan. "How's your story about the festival coming?"

Though she hesitated for a moment and gave Maris a quick glance, the hawkish look turned softer as she smiled at Spats. "It turns out that it's all about the personalities, past and present." She was tentative at first, but gained some momentum. "From the woman who started the festival because of her love of the blues, to the people who actually play it; people from every walk of life brought together for one purpose–"

"Great music," Maris interjected, smiling.

"Great wine," Bowdie said, lifting his glass.

"Great digs," Spats added, lifting his glass too.

"Great food," George agreed, and lifted his plate. Everyone laughed with the big man.

Megan finally lifted her glass as well. "To the musicians who made it possible," she said, and everyone drank with her.

Maris eyed her retired guest for a moment. "I wonder if everyone knows that George is a musician as well."

"What?" Spats said. He turned to the big man. "You play?"

George seemed to shrink a little under the sudden attention. "I used to."

Maris put down her wine, went to him, and put a hand on his shoulder. "False modesty, I'm afraid. George was kind enough to play for Cookie, Mojo, and I the other day."

"So you're holding out on us," Bowdie said. "What do you play?"

George smiled a bit shyly. "Piano."

"Blues piano," Maris added.

Spats set down his plate. "Well let's hear some."

"Oh, I wouldn't want to make you–"

Bowdie stepped forward. "We've been playing all day, man. It'd be great to listen."

George looked around the room. "Well, if you insist..."

"We do," Maris said.

In a few moments they had all moved to the parlor, where George sat down and began to play. It was an upbeat tune, quick and peppy, that Maris seemed to recognize. Spats immediately beamed at Bowdie and the two men stepped closer to the piano. Heads bopped and toes tapped as the brief intro led into the song.

"Got my mojo working," the three men sang, "but it just won't work on you. Got my mojo working but it just won't work on you."

Maris joined in as well. "Got my mojo working but it just won't work on you."

Just then Mojo appeared in the doorway, and Maris went to pick him up, singing, "I want to love you so bad." She hugged the fluffy black cat close. "But I just don't know what to do."

Although Megan grinned at Mojo, the men hadn't seen him, concentrating on the song. As they belted out the rest of the verse, Bowdie sang a harmony and Spats began to clap in time. George's fingers flew over the keyboard, and it was over all too soon.

Applause erupted and Mojo meowed his signature sound in appreciation, making everyone laugh.

Bowdie and Spats patted George on the shoulders.

"We've got a natural here," Spats said.

Bowdie nodded. "We make a good band," he declared.

Spats thought for a moment, as George

swiveled around. "You know what, I think we do."

"I'd have to agree," Megan said. "That was pretty nice."

"A small band can be tight," Bowdie said, the gears turning behind his eyes. He looked down at the still seated piano player. "You know what I mean?"

The big man nodded. "Oh, definitely. A band's got to gel. If the magic isn't there, it just isn't."

The younger guitarist nodded. "That's exactly what I was thinking."

"Takes more than musicianship," Spats agreed. He glanced at Maris. "We can all play our part, but it takes real teamwork to pull off a song that sounds so together."

Maris smiled at him. "I never thought of that."

"Say, George," Bowdie said to him. "You wouldn't be interested in maybe getting together with me and Spats for a little studio time, would you?"

George seemed to be bursting at the seams. "You bet I would. I haven't seen the inside of a studio for decades."

Megan had taken one of the napkins and

clicked her pen. When Maris glanced at her, she said, "Just want to note the date, the time, and the place." She lowered her voice. "I think we might just have seen the birth of something special."

Mojo squirmed to be put down and trotted immediately over to George, who patted his lap. "Come on up, little fella."

"Let's do another," Spats said. "George, you want to start us off?"

Mojo remained in the big man's lap as he turned to the piano and started playing.

Maris had to smile. Megan could be right. They might be witnessing the start of the next big blues band.

But as she watched the trio, her thoughts went unexpectedly back to the thefts. Something in the back of her mind, suddenly jumped to the front, and she understood why the missing items had made no sense. More importantly, she knew who was responsible for the larceny. She smiled even wider. Tomorrow was going to be an interesting day.

30

The next morning was a whirlwind of activity. After breakfast, the guests had all departed, with fervent wishes for a return visit next year. Maris and Cookie worked until noon stripping the beds and bathrooms and putting on fresh linens. Though new guests weren't expected for a couple of days, they both liked to see the B&B looking good.

"An unmade bed..." Cookie said, as she took up the fresh towels, passing Maris on the stairs.

"Is a messy bed," Maris said, taking down the trash.

In her hospitality career, she had always been a stickler for having everything in readiness. Though their next guests might not be expected until later in the week, now they were ready for a traveler who might simply be stopping by. The bonus was knowing that everything was neat and tidy as well.

Once the upstairs was ready, they met in the kitchen.

"I think I'll skip the dusting and vacuuming today," Maris said, taking a seat at the butcher block.

Cookie was heating some water for tea. "Me too," she said. "There are some plants in the garden that are feeling pretty neglected."

Maris glanced toward the back. "Is Bear working today?"

"I don't think so," Cookie said. She poured the hot water into the two waiting china cups. "Why do you ask?" She brought the cups over and took a seat as well.

Maris accepted one of the cups. "Thank you. That smells wonderful." She inhaled the wonderful aroma of chamomile deeply. "I've got an errand in town and thought I'd pick up lunch from Flour Power."

Cookie smiled, wrapping her hands around the cup. "I'm sure he'll be sorry to miss that." She took a sip of her tea and set it back on the block. "But one of Fab's sand-wiches sounds, well, fab."

Maris sipped her tea as well. It had just the right amount of Bear's honey. She smiled at the diminutive chef. "I couldn't have said it better myself."

"What are you doing in town?"

Maris set her cup down. "I'll be catching a thief."

SITTING in the circle with the others, Maris took the potholder from her canvas bag. The other ladies all peered at it for a moment, before returning to their own work.

"Another potholder?" Zarina asked, leaning forward. Her huge glasses were a vi-brant purple today, matching the floral head scarf.

Maris flushed a little. "No. Same one."

"Ah," said the plump woman, settling back with a little smile.

"You know," Eunice said, putting her cro-chet project in her lap, "if you worked on that at home too, you might actually finish it."

"Now, now, Eunice," Millicent said

smoothly. "We're not all as blazingly fast as you, you know."

Maris only smiled at the the older woman with the too red hair. "I've been a bit busy."

"Oh heavens," said Helen, as she continued work on her doily. "Haven't we all been? But the festival was another great success."

"Better every year," Vera agreed. She moved her glasses up her nose a bit to look out the front window. "I don't know how the plaza could have held any more people."

"I wasn't busy with the festival," Maris said to no one in particular. "Or the B&B. No, I was busy figuring out who stole all the missing items."

As one, everyone stopped crocheting, and yet no one lifted their gaze. Maris suppressed a knowing smile as she recalled how quickly Millicent and Eunice had implicated the journalist, and also Claribel's remote vision of the president of the club.

It was Millicent who finally broke the awkward silence. "And have you?" she asked, her tone almost bored.

Maris let the potholder rest in her lap. "It

was you," she replied. She let her glance take in the entire circle. "All of you."

Eventually everyone's work slowly lowered and their gazes went to Millicent, who then calmly looked at Maris. "Well, I suppose there's really no point in denying it."

"No," Maris said. "There isn't. But what I don't know is why?"

A flurry of looks were exchanged, but Maris simply waited. Millicent nodded to Helen, who cleared her throat.

"As an earth elemental," she said, "I was in charge of taking Howard's crystal ball." She snapped her fingers. "Easiest thing in the world to get it."

Maris's eyebrows arched at the revelation. For a moment, she could only sit, stunned. She'd run into Helen outside the market that day before the festival. But as she thought of that morning, and poor Howard when he'd found his crystal ball was gone, she said, "Will he be getting it back?"

Helen shook her head, smiling. "You'll let him know he needs a new one?"

Maris frowned at the incongruous smile. "Sure."

The elderly woman waved a hand at her. "Oh it was cracked anyway. He'd do better with a new one."

"I'm a gravity elemental," Zarina said. "Did you know?" When Maris shook her head, she said, "I took the fishing weights from Ryan Quigg's shop."

"Okay," Maris said quietly, feeling a bit bewildered.

"Air elemental," Vera said, holding up her hand as though she was swearing an oath. "Aurora will discover that she's missing some wind chimes."

Maris looked at Eunice, who actually smiled for a change. "I'm a fire elemental," the older woman said. "I took some gasoline from Flour Power. The honey from Bear was just a bonus."

"But we like him," Millicent added, "so we decided to keep it."

"You like him," Maris echoed, trying to puzzle it out. "And that's why you'll keep it." She frowned a little as the ladies all grinned at her. If they liked someone, they stole from them? Then she recalled the credit card machine.

"And Eugene?"

Millicent chuckled a little. "Oh, that was all him. We didn't take his credit card machine. He misplaced it. Delia found it at their booth in the plaza. We took one of their menus."

"So that means you like Eugene?" Maris asked.

"And his daughter," Vera declared. "Goodness, what a cook!"

Maris regarded Eunice. "And your phone that went missing?"

The thin woman shrugged. "That was a lie. No one took it."

Maris's mouth dropped open a little. They'd lied to her?

"If anyone was going to figure it out," Millicent said, "we knew it'd be you." Heads bobbed all around the circle. "A little misdirection was in order."

"Right," Maris said quietly. "Right."

She'd already figured out the missing blues album. Watching a musician who needed to protect his hands, but who had then worked on his car's engine, hadn't made sense. Nor did his bling match the way he'd wolfed down the lunch that Mac had bought, or the way that the wine and cheese was clearly dinner. He'd taken the album, likely for its value, but had then returned it.

"We got a little behind this year," Millicent said. "So we decided to use the festival as cover. It only made sense that, with the town swamped with tourists, that the thefts could be attributed to them."

Maris gazed at the faces all around her. "Got behind on what? On stealing?" She paused and thought for a moment. "And why are you all stealing these things in the first place?" It felt as though she'd wandered into a kleptomania club, or maybe an alternate universe.

All eyes went to Millicent, who said, "Perhaps you'd like to join us this evening, just past sunset."

More looks were exchanged, but also grins.

Maris's brows knit together but she smiled. "Um, I'd be delighted. Here?"

Millicent nodded. "Yes, here, just after sunset. Make sure to dress warm." She and the other ladies returned to their crocheting.

Then the club president added, "And bring something from the B&B." She gave Maris a little wink. "Something you wouldn't mind losing."

31

Just after sunset, Maris returned to Millicent's home, only to find the group assembled in front. After the hectic days of the festival, the plaza seemed particularly empty but also quite peaceful. The ladies were all wearing sweaters, as was Maris. She'd also made sure to bring the tiny potted plant with her. Although Cookie had no more idea what the crochet club had planned, they both felt that the little bunch of sage from the herb garden would not only be fragrant, but encompass the soothing and calming effect that they hoped their hospitality had on their guests.

As Maris joined them on the sidewalk, they looked at what she'd brought.

"Perfect," Millicent declared. "Shall we go?"

Maris glanced around at them. "Go where?"

Zarina took her by the elbow. "Not far. You'll see."

The six of them piled into two cars, Zarina and Vera driving. Maris decided to simply wait and see what was happening and where they were going. But when they exited Pixie Point Bay and headed east, she hazarded a guess. They were headed toward the redwoods. Millicent had told her to dress warmly, and now she was glad she'd done exactly that. In just thirty minutes, they were at the entrance to a trailhead.

As Zarina parked the car, she said, "It's just a twenty minute walk from here." She reached into the glove compartment and took out two small flashlights. "You'll need this later," she said, handing one to Maris.

"Thanks," Maris said, and the two of them got out and joined the others.

As on the drive over, there was no chit chat. Though the mood wasn't somber or strained in the least, Maris sensed some underlying reason for the quiet. But as they made their way along the path in the growing darkness, the group finally seemed to have arrived somewhere. One by one they stepped over the low stones that lined the dirt path, and went into the trees. Zarina motioned for Maris to precede her.

Only a few dozen yards from the path, they entered a clearing. Looking back, Maris could no longer see the official trail, let alone the parking lot. One by one the ladies all gathered around what looked like a small teepee of wood logs. Maris realized with a start, that it was the makings of a fire, and recalled her precognitive vision.

Millicent pointed at the wood. "You can put your plant in there."

When Maris stepped forward with it, she got a whiff of gasoline and then saw some familiar objects among the logs. The crystal ball was there, along with Bear's jar of honey, and a menu from the smokehouse. In fact, there had to be dozens of objects, most of them small. The club had to have been collecting them for some time. She wedged the small pot in between a couple of the logs.

As she returned to her place in the circle, she recalled the tarot card, the five of pentacles, and gazed at the five other women. Mojo had been right again.

"Good," Millicent said. "You'll want to keep back." She turned to Eunice. "Would you do the honors?"

The thin older lady stepped forward, bent over the pile of wood, and reached her hand to it. Tiny, multi-colored flames leapt from her fingers and landed on the gasoline soaked wood. The fire began immediately.

Eunice stepped back and Maris worried for a moment that these ladies might not know what they were doing, lighting a fire among the trees. Yet everything about the moment seemed, not only natural, but something well rehearsed—or at least done many times.

"This is the Five-Fold Blessing," Millicent said to her. "We'll call upon all the elements, and offer up our many gathered prizes, as we entreat them to bless Pixie Point Bay for another year."

"Five-fold," Maris repeated, thinking back to the Ouija board.

Without prompting, Eunice turned to the east and raised her hands.

"Element of fire, accept our offerings,

Gathered with love for your safekeeping, Keep our community safe and well, And we shall not forget to count our blessings."

Helen was next, as she turned to the south. "Element of earth, accept our offerings, Gathered with love for your safekeeping, Keep our community safe and well, And we shall not forget to count our blessings."

Zarina made the same entreaty to gravity, facing west, and Vera entreated air to the north.

Maris listened to each one in turn as the flickering flames lit their faces. The gentle light smoothed out the deep wrinkles and melted away the years. As the scent of woodsmoke wafted around them, the fire quietly crackled.

Finally Millicent raised her hands to the sky. "Element of aether, accept our offerings, Gathered with love for your safekeeping, Keep our community safe and well, And we shall not forget to count our blessings."

As the last of her words faded, and the embers of the fire slowly rose, silence descended on the group. A deep feeling of peace settled over Maris, and for a moment she thought she could smell the sage. The centuries old trees that soared all around them, seemed to be keeping a silent watch. Above them, barely visible through the canopy, a few stars had managed to peek through.

She thought of the town, all the businesses, and all her friends. How lucky she was to have found her home here. As she gazed around at the smiling faces, she couldn't help but nod to herself. She too would remember to count her blessings, and not just once a year.

The Witch Who Saw a Murder

Excerpt

CHAPTER ONE

Maris carried the blanket, Bear carried the basket, and Cookie brought the thermoses. Though the Towne Plaza was enormous, it was starting to look like the beach in summer, with colorful ground coverings and coolers everywhere.

"Goodness," Maris said. "I didn't realize Pixie Point Bay Picnic Day was going to be so popular."

"They always are," Cookie said, smiling and looking around. Her bright floral dress matched the surroundings perfectly. "I haven't been to one of these in years."

It wasn't often that Ruth "Cookie" Calderon came to town at all. The B&B's chef always said that she preferred home—particularly her kitchen and garden—to just about anywhere.

Picnic Day, however, was an exception.

"How about here?" Maris asked her companions. She came to a stop and surveyed the neatly trimmed patch of grass about midway to the Oriental gazebo.

"Fine by me," the diminutive chef said, looking at her, and then up at Bear.

Their outsized handyman grinned at her. "Looks good."

He easily stood two heads above them and carried the heavily laden picnic basket as though it was a lunchbox. His neatly trimmed beard didn't hide his smile. Nor did his bib overalls hide a burgeoning paunch at the midriff.

"Great," Maris said, and unfurled the checkered blanket.

"Is that the new pizzeria?" Cookie asked, looking in its direction.

Located in a building that was even narrower than the medical clinic, wedged between Castaways and Superior Hardware, was the newest establishment in town: Pizza del Popolo.

Maris glanced in that direction as she continued to spread out the blanket. "That's the one," she confirmed.

Cookie nodded. "It's about time."

Bear sniffed the air. "I can smell it." He arched his heavy brows. "It smells good."

Satisfied with the blanket, Maris gazed in the pizzeria's direction. "I'm happy to say it tastes good too." Bear swiveled his head back to her. "He's having his soft opening this week, and I was invited for a sample." She grinned at him. "It's good to be the owner of the Pixie Point Bay Lighthouse and B&B."

Not only was it her job to ensure the comfort of her guests, but they often asked for restaurant recommendations. She regularly sampled new menu offerings, even at places she'd eaten many times.

"Shall we have a seat?" Cookie said. As she sat down on the blanket, Bear placed the basket next to her. "Thank you, Bear."

Maris paused to scan the area. "Oh, there he is," she said, and waved.

Mac saw her, waved back, and headed their way. She watched him stride over. It always pleased her to see him dressed in something other than his uniform. Six feet tall and athletically built, Sheriff McKenna of Medio County had the kind of rugged good looks that made hearts flutter. His gray eyes and matching salt and pepper hair only added to his charm.

She held out her hands to him as he approached. He took them and leaned in for a quick peck on the cheek.

"I'm glad you could make it," Maris said.

"I wouldn't have missed it," he replied before pulling away and looking down at her. "You look lovely."

She'd made sure to wear the most flattering skirt and blouse that she owned, and had taken extra time with her hair. Despite having aimed for exactly that compliment, heat rose to her cheeks. "Thank you."

Mac nodded to the chef. "Cookie. It's good to see you."

Cookie had opened the basket, but paused, smiling as she shielded her eyes from the sun. "Nice to see you too, Sheriff."

He reached across Maris and offered his

hand to Bear. "Good morning, Bear. How's it going?"

"Very well, Mac," he said, shaking the sheriff's hand. "And you?"

Mac grinned at him, and then at Maris. "Never better."

Bear gave him a little nod as he nimbly descended into a cross-legged position, facing Cookie. Not as light as the chef nor as young as their handyman, Maris took her time getting to the ground, with a helping hand from Mac. Since arriving back in Pixie Point Bay she felt more healthy than she had in decades. With her weight steadily if slowly dropping, she expected that her cholesterol would be getting to a good range too. But it didn't mean she was any more limber. When she finally sat down, Mac joined her, and Cookie started to unpack the basket.

"Maris, would you pour the tea please?" She handed her the plastic mugs, and then a thermos.

"My pleasure," Maris said. She'd just been unscrewing the plastic top when a voice assailed her from behind.

"Maris," he said. "*Ciao, Bella!*"

Before she turned her head, she had to

smile. "Massimo," she said, seeing him approach. "Oh!" she exclaimed. He was barreling toward them with a stack of pizza boxes in his arms.

In his early fifties, the owner of the new pizzeria wasn't particularly a big man but he'd impressed Maris as 'solid.' The hint of a beard at the jaw line and his short mustache were only flecked with gray. But his hair—shaved close at the sides and combed back on top—was a lustrous chestnut brown. The short haircut emphasized the one cauliflower ear, and Maris had previously noticed his bent nose.

As he reached the blanket, he quickly crouched and set down the pizzas. Kneeling next to her, he leaned closer for an air kiss on one cheek, then the other.

"How wonderful to see you," he said. Without waiting for introductions, he extended a hand to Cookie. "I am Massimo Cuore, but please call me Max."

She smiled at him as they shook. "Cookie Calderon."

He paused, his mouth open in shock as he glanced at Maris. "The chef?" Maris smiled and nodded. He took Cookie's hand in both of his and gave her a little bow. "It is an honor to finally meet you. I have heard about you...*everywhere*."

"Oh, well," Cookie said, her face flushing pink. "That's very kind." She glanced down at their hands, looking more flustered than Maris had ever seen the older woman.

"Oh, pardon!" he said, and let her hand go. "I am in disbelief that I am actually meeting you."

When the diminutive chef seemed lost for words, Maris said, "And this is Sheriff Daniel McKenna."

Mac shook the chef's hand. "We've actually already met," the sheriff said. "Good to see you."

"You've met?" Maris asked.

Max nodded. "At the County Recorders office." He grinned at Mac. "I was lost but luckily the sheriff found me."

It was no wonder that the crows feet at the corners of Max's dark eyes were deep because, as always, his smile was enormous. As usual he wore a traditional white chef's shirt, but modified with a stripe of bright green running down one side of his chest, and a stripe of red down the other.

"And may I introduce Bear Orsino." She gestured to the big man. "The world's most accomplished handyman."

Max thrust his hand forward, peering into Bear's face. "Orsino? From the old country?"

Bear took the man's hand. "Abruzzo. My grandfather."

Max slapped his other hand over Bear's enormous one and shook it vigorously. "Ho, *compagno!*" he exclaimed, beaming. "My family too. Maybe near Matelica?"

Bear shook his head but grinned. "Pioraco."

"Oh, the mountains!" He regarded the young man. "Fitting. Very fitting."

"Massimo," Maris said. "Would you–"

"Please call me Max," he said, putting on a hurt look. "We are friends, are we not?"

Maris laughed a little. "Max," she started again, "would you like to join us?"

He put a hand over his heart as he sat back on his heels. "I am honored. Truly." Then he reached to the boxes of pizza, took one, and handed it to her. "But I am on my tour of the plaza. Free pizza for everyone."

Maris cocked her head back as she accepted it. "Free pizza?"

Cookie added, "For everyone?" She gazed around at the plaza.

"Yes," he said, nodding. Then he stood. "So I best go on my way." He took them all in with a fond look. "It was a pleasure to meet you."

Maris opened the box top and took a peek. The beautiful smell of the tomato sauce and fresh crust immediately wafted up.

"A seafood pizza?" she said, as Max bent and picked up the rest of the boxes.

He grinned down at her. "When in Roma, eh?" Then he was off, heading toward the next blanket. "*Ciao, amici!*"

"Look at that," Cookie said, gazing down into the box with awe in her voice. "Are those scallops?"

"And baby shrimp and crab meat," Mac said nodding.

"I can smell the garlic," Bear said.

Maris was about to set the box down so they could all take a slice, but then she remembered the basket. Cookie had spent the morning getting their picnic ready.

When the chef noticed her gaze, she closed and patted its wicker top. "It'll keep." Then she eyed the pizza. "Let's give this a try."

Maris quickly set the box down and they each took a slice. Bear folded his piece and was the first to take a bite. "Mmm hmm," he murmured.

Maris had already sampled Max's triple mushroom pizza earlier in the week. But as she took her first bite, she knew immediately that this was completely different. He'd changed the tomato sauce to compliment the seafood—just a tad on the zesty side.

Mac nodded as he chewed. He gave Maris the thumbs up sign.

Cookie was next. As the chef sampled her slice, Maris saw the gears turning behind the dark and glittering eyes. She covered her mouth as she said, "Oh, that is good." She looked down at her slice, analyzing it. "Asiago instead of Parmesan. Very nice choice. It's–"

"Pig!" said a woman's shrill voice. "Chauvinist pig!"

Not ten yards away, a woman was shaking her fist at someone.

"Who is that?" Maris asked. She didn't recognize either of them.

"Rudy Schmid," Bear said.

"The owner of Superior Hardware," Cookie said, glaring at him with distaste. She peered at the pair a while longer before returning to her pizza. "I don't know the woman."

The tall man standing in front of her, on what was presumably his blanket, had his arms folded over his chest and was laughing. He shook his head and said something Maris couldn't make out. The woman was so angry that she was shaking.

Maris looked back at Bear and Cookie, who were eating their pizza, making her frown. "Wait a minute," she said, reluctantly setting her slice down, just as Mac did. "That woman just called him a pig, and is obviously livid. Am I the only one bothered about it?"

Bear shrugged. "It's Rudy." He took another bite.

Cookie nodded. "He is a pig."

Maris stared at her. "What?"

"That's it!" the woman screamed. As Maris watched, she spun on her heel, stalked off—and tripped.

"Oh no," Maris said, as the angry woman went down in a pile. Thank goodness they were on grass. She must have tripped on someone's blanket.

Mac shot to his feet but a young man nearby went over to help her up. But when he bent over her, he crouched down. His panicked face, as he scanned the plaza, said everything.

"Ambulance," he yelled. "Someone get an ambulance!"

• • • • •

Buy The Witch Who Saw a Murder

FREE BOOK

If you'd like to learn how Maris arrived in Pixie Point Bay and got her start, you can read *The Witch Who Saw the Light* for FREE by signing up for my newsletter at the link below.

Get A Free Book

DEDICATION

For Mr. Bee's Knees

COPYRIGHT

tion of this book via the Internet or via any other means without the permission of the copyright owner is illegal. Please purchase only authorized electronic editions, and do not participate in or encourage electronic piracy of copyrighted materials. Your support of the author's rights is appreciated.

9 781950 575251